"Let Go Of Me, Rush."

But she lamented the huskiness in her voice, because what had been intended as a demand came out sounding like an invitation.

If only he wasn't so handsome, so damned male, Val thought wildly, finding herself staring into shimmering blue eyes. He tugged on her arm, just a little, and she took a tiny step toward him.

His free hand rose to her other arm, and he pulled her forward, very slowly. Then both of his hands rose to her hair, and she saw the muscles in his jaw clench as he wove his fingers into it.

"Fantastic," he mumbled thickly. "Don't ever pin it back again, please."

She swallowed. Move! Get away from him! she told herself.

But her shoes felt glued to the floor, and the sensation of his hands in her hair was making her dizzy.

Dear Reader,

Every month we try to bring you something exciting in Silhouette Desire, and this month is no exception.

First, there's the *Man of the Month* by Jennifer Greene, which *also* is the start of a charming new miniseries by this award-winning writer. The book is *Bewitched* and the series is called JOCK'S BOYS after the delightful, meddlesome ghost of an old sea pirate.

Next, Jackie Merritt's sinfully sexy series about the Saxon Brothers continues with *Mystery Lady*. Here, brother Rush Saxon meets his match in alluring ice princess Valentine LeClaire.

Lass Small hasn't run out of Brown siblings yet! In *I'm Gonna Get You*, Tom Brown learns that you can't always get who you want when you want her....

Suzanne Simms has always been asked by her friends, "Why don't you write some funny books?" So, Suzanne decided to try and *The Brainy Beauty*—the first book in her HAZARDS, INC. series—is the fun-filled result.

And so you don't think that miniseries books are the only thing we do, look for *Rafferty's Angel* by up-and-coming writer Caroline Cross. And don't miss Donna Carlisle's *Stealing Savannah*, about a suave ex-jewel thief and the woman who's out to get him.

Sincerely,

Lucia Macro
Senior Editor

JACKIE MERRITT
MYSTERY LADY

SILHOUETTE *Desire*®
Published by Silhouette Books
America's Publisher of Contemporary Romance

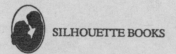

SILHOUETTE BOOKS

ISBN 0-373-05849-7

MYSTERY LADY

JACKIE MERRITT

and her husband live just outside of Las Vegas, Nevada. An accountant for many years, Jackie has happily traded numbers for words. Next to family, books are her greatest joy. She started writing in 1987 and her efforts paid off in 1988 with the publication of her first novel. When she's not writing or enjoying a good book, Jackie dabbles in watercolor painting and has been known to tickle the ivories in her spare time.

Prologue

Rush Saxon telephoned his brothers, Cash and Chance, and suggested dinner together that evening. "Just to talk," he told them. Stating the obvious wasn't necessary. All three men knew they might not have an opportunity to sit down at the same table for a long time, once they actually left New York for their various destinations.

A week had passed since the Saxon brothers had met with Robert Teale, the Saxon family attorney, and heard the news that dramatically changed their lives. The death of their beloved granddad hadn't yet been digested when Teale called the meeting to relate, calmly and sympathetically, that there was very little in Gerald Saxon's estate to pass on to his grandsons.

The shock of being close to penniless when they were accustomed to living with everything money could buy was beginning to abate after a week. To their credit, the Saxon brothers weren't sitting around lamenting the loss of the only life-style they knew. They had made a quick and sen-

sible decision, to take what was left, three financially
strapped businesses in three different states, and get on with
their lives.

Chance, the eldest, was going to Montana to the Kidd
River Cattle Ranch; Cash was heading for a logging company in Oregon; and Rush, the youngest, was planning to
assume possession of a house construction·company in Las
Vegas, Nevada.

Rush hosted the small dinner party in a favorite restaurant. "Call it a last hurrah," he said jokingly to his older
brothers, referring to the cost of the meal.

After laughing about the crack, the trio fell silent. They
had eaten and enjoyed a fine dinner, and had talked about
everything but their upcoming ventures throughout the
courses, from boyhood pranks to college days to recent
travels.

They were a handsome group, exceptionally well dressed,
tall and lean and dark haired, bearing marked similarities in
facial features. Any stranger would have known they were
closely related from their heavily lashed, vivid blue eyes, if
nothing else. They were young, thirty, thirty-two and thirty-
four, and most importantly, they liked each other. Losing
their parents to a plane crash twenty-nine years ago had
created a strong bond between them. They all knew how
fortunate they had been to have their grandfather not only
take them in, but love them.

Over fresh coffee they spoke respectfully of Gerald
Saxon, recalling treasured moments from the past, laughing about some, choking up over others.

Finally they began talking about their departure dates,
which were coming up in a matter of days. Behind each pair
of blue eyes lay unspoken concern and a raw edge of uncertainty. They were heading into an unknown future and each
was aware of it.

"Are you two going to be all right?" Chance asked quietly.

"I was thinking the same thing about you two," Cash said.

Rush sat back and smiled. "And I was worrying about the two of you."

They looked at each other with fond amazement, then laughed: Clearly each man was a lot more worried about his brothers than himself.

"Guess what, gang," Rush said in an unashamedly emotional voice. "I think we're going to make it."

They lifted their coffee cups to the center of the table and touched the china together in mute agreement.

The emotional moment passed when the waiter appeared with the check. Rush insisted on paying, and the brothers walked out together.

"Let's get together for a drink or something one more time," Chance said. "How about two nights from now?"

Each was glad to delay their final farewell, and the time and place were quickly decided upon.

Then they walked away to go their separate ways. Internally, each man's worry for the other two hadn't completely disappeared, but all three felt a little better. The Saxon brothers, after all, weren't lacking in intelligence. What was energizing for each to realize was that neither were they lacking in flexibility.

Only time would tell if brains and a willingness to roll with the punches were enough.

One

Rush Saxon's flight landed at McCarron International Airport at 7:20 p.m. He collected his luggage, rented a car and bought a street map of Las Vegas. His first surprise was the city's size on the map. During his one other visit to the gambling capital, he had stayed on the Strip and never realized there was an honest-to-gosh city beyond it.

The evening temperature was in the eighties and fabulous. Rush studied the map, made mental notes and then drove with the windows down, following Paradise Street to Tropicana, where he veered left and headed for the Strip. The massive hotels created a spectacular skyline, which he enjoyed seeing.

But he was looking at Las Vegas from a much different perspective than his previous weekend visit, Rush reminded himself. This was his home now, as strange as it felt. His future was committed to a construction business he'd never seen, never heard of until recently, and had no idea how to run.

Rush openly admitted his own preference for the best of everything. His expensive tastes had been coddled and gratified all of his life. The gold watch on his wrist was an exquisite Piaget; his luggage was Louis Vuitton; and the loafers on his feet had been custom-made at Maxwell's in London at a cost of eleven hundred dollars.

"How the mighty have fallen," Rush said under his breath with an amused little half smile. Not that the situation was anything but serious, but he was determined to approach this new and startling phase of his life with an open mind, and the fact that the "mighty had indeed fallen" was about as blatantly honest as any thought he'd ever had.

Rush followed the Strip to downtown Las Vegas, then found a parking space near a small hotel-casino and went inside for a cup of coffee. He spread the map out on the table and marked some streets and routes with his pen while he drank two cups. With the map folded and in his pocket again, he left the coffee shop and walked through the casino to the front door.

The place was jumping. Smiling, Rush stopped to watch some dollar slot players who were winning and having a ball. The action of the place was entertaining, but he couldn't waste any of his small cache of money on gambling. Besides, he had to find a place to stay for the night, preferably a quiet motel in the vicinity of the construction company's office.

It took nearly an hour to locate the office and then the motel. He hauled in his luggage and then returned to his car, to drive back to the company office for a preliminary visit. He'd been given a set of keys by Teale, the attorney, and a packet of files and papers a foot deep. "Information and reports about the company, Rush," Teale had told him. "Look them over. They'll familiarize you with the business."

Rush had done some looking on the plane, but had gained little beyond a confusing barrage of meaningless figures. There'd been a few helpful facts: The company was presently engaged in the construction of a single-family housing development—the Saxon Springs project—consisting of one hundred and ten units with five different floor plans and prices.

Driving up to the office again, he was surprised to see lights on inside and a car parked near the door. As everything had been dark a short time ago, he wondered who the caller was.

He parked next to the blue sedan and got out. Lights spilled across the walkway from two large front windows. He stopped near one to peer in, and frowned slightly when he saw a woman seated at one of the desks. She was in profile, wearing jeans and a white blouse. Her hair was a great color, sun-streaked blond, but it was trussed up in a severe knot, and there was a pair of glasses perched on her nose. She was about his age, Rush reckoned, maybe a little older, and seemed engrossed in the papers on the desk in front of her.

He moved to the door and tried the knob, thinking it would turn. Surprised to find it locked, he rapped.

Val jumped two feet. No one that she knew of ever came to the office at night. She got up. "Who is it?"

"Rush Saxon."

Saxon? Since Val's association with the Saxon Construction Company, she hadn't met a Saxon, let alone had one come along without warning and after dark. Uncertain about this, she uneasily moved to the door. "Do you have some ID?"

"What?"

"Do you have some ID?"

Impatiently Rush pulled out his wallet and then his driver's license. He walked to the window and flattened it against the glass. "Will this do?"

Val gingerly approached the window glass and took a look at the license. It said Rush Saxon, and the photo was a bad likeness of the handsome man peering at her through the window. Glowering at her, actually.

She didn't care if he glowered or not. Her motto was better safe than sorry, and there were a lot of seedy characters roaming the streets.

Returning to the door, she unlocked then opened it. "I don't usually see anyone when I'm here at night," she said as Rush walked in shoving his wallet into the back pocket of his slacks.

"What are you doing here?" he questioned bluntly.

"I needed to go over some files."

"Do you work here?"

"I'm associated with the business. I've been selling the houses at the Saxon Springs project."

"Oh, you're a real estate agent."

"Yes."

Rush looked around. The office was of modest size and without a hint of any planned decor, merely three desks arranged in no particular pattern, each bearing a telephone. There were several file cabinets. The floor was covered with a nondescript beige carpet. The walls were plain white and adorned with large maps, layouts of the project, he assumed, and a couple of calendars. Oh yes, there was a marvelous six-foot tall ficus tree near a window, the only saving grace in the rather dismal little office.

Val was thinking that Mr. Rush Saxon looked a lot more like a playboy than the owner of a construction company. Those were Armani slacks on his remarkable physique, she'd be willing to bet, and custom-made loafers on his feet. His watch was gorgeous, worth ten thousand at the very least.

He was maybe the best-looking guy she'd ever seen, and she'd seen plenty of good-looking guys. Saxon's skin was the perfect shade of tan, and his eyes were so blue they seemed piercing. His hair, which he wore on the longish side contrary to current style, was lush and lustrous, nearly black, bearing a slight wave that didn't prevent it from shaping to his head in a most beguiling manner.

She kept her expression aloof while he took in the office, but she wouldn't be very female if she didn't notice such an outstanding specimen of masculinity. In her case, a little admiration never went beyond that. Or it didn't anymore. There was a time when her head had been turned by perfect features and an impressive build on a man, but no more. These days she preferred solidity and intelligence over good looks.

Rush turned back to the woman. "What's your name?"

"Val LeClair."

"How many units have you sold?"

"Eighty-seven. That's seventy-nine percent of the project, Mr. Saxon."

"Rush. If we're going to be working together, let's not stand on formality."

Val raised an eyebrow. "Are we going to be working together?"

"Seems so." Rush walked over to one of the desks. "Are these all being used?"

"Not anymore. That one was used by Dirk Johnson, the project manager. He walked off the job about two weeks ago."

Rush frowned. "He walked off? Did he say why?"

"He said a lot of things, but the crux of his complaints was that there was no money to finish the project. Mr. Saxon...Rush...not one house at Saxon Springs has been completed. My buyers are getting impatient, and I'm afraid we're going to lose them." Val was beginning to feel a welcome relief. The project was in a dangerous limbo at the present, and she'd invested an enormous amount of time and energy in its sales program. A Saxon showing up had to mean certain rescue; after all, she'd heard repeatedly from Dirk Johnson how wealthy the family was, and all the project really needed was money.

Rush walked around, slowly, looking at the displays on the walls, touching a leaf on the ficus tree, returning to the desk. He was thinking hard. Having no project manager was unsettling, as Johnson had been the liaison between the construction people and himself. Now what?

"The construction crews are grumbling, as well," Val continued. "Some of them are leaving the project for steadier work." She was watching Rush Saxon, seeking his reaction. Actually, other than seventy-nine percent of the project being sold, she had little that was good to tell him.

Everything she said drove the knife a little deeper in Rush's gut. He had to hear it all, though. "We're short-handed, then?"

"I'm not certain of the logistics, Rush, but when I was on the site earlier today, only a few carpenters were working. Frankly, with no one to sign their paychecks, it's a wonder anyone was there."

"Johnson signed the checks?"

"I believe he did. My involvement with the company only goes so far, you must understand. There are records in this office I've never seen, which is normal." Val sighed quietly, disliking the role of bearer of bad tidings. But who else was there to fill in Rush Saxon? "Other than the sales of the houses, which I know inside and out, my information is based on what others have told me."

"Other people's complaints."

"Yes, I'm afraid so." Val walked over to her desk and sat down. She had to leave in a very few minutes, and she began closing file folders.

Rush understood her actions to be a prologue to leaving. "I'd appreciate it if you'd stay a little longer," he said politely.

Val removed her reading glasses and put them into their case. "I wish I could, but I have to..." No, she decided then and there. What she did outside of Saxon company business was none of this man's affair. "I have an appointment I can't break," she finished firmly. "But I can be here tomorrow."

Rush's gaze rested on Val LeClair's face. She had nice features, a small nose, a full mouth, a perfect complexion, large brown eyes. But there wasn't a sign of makeup on her face, and that awful hairdo, pulled straight back from her forehead and temples, did absolutely nothing for her looks. He simply could not accurately judge her age, he decided, though it had to be somewhere between thirty and thirty-five. She was taller than average and reed-thin, though the swells of her breasts in that unflattering blouse weren't to be denied. Her jeans were old and faded almost white, clinging to her slender hips and long thighs, and on her feet were a pair of ancient canvas shoes.

With a decent hairdo, good clothes and some makeup, she could be a striking woman, he thought. He couldn't believe she sold real estate looking like this. He figured she'd run by the office without worrying about her appearance because she was certain no one would come along.

Still, she hadn't gotten at all flustered when he showed up, as a lot of women would have, fluttering and apologizing because they didn't look their best. Rush knew most women noticed him as a man, but Val LeClair hadn't and apparently still didn't.

He wasn't normally focused on his ego, but there was something subtly annoying about Val's uninterested attitude. Of course, she could be married or involved, or simply not drawn to the opposite sex.

Clearing his throat, he walked to the door with her. She had slung the long strap of her purse over her left shoulder, and carried her car keys in her right hand.

"Shall I count on your being here tomorrow morning?" she asked.

"I'll be here," Rush stated flatly.

"In that case, I'll see you then. Good night."

When she was gone and even the taillights of her car had disappeared, Rush plopped down at one of the vacant desks. An unfamiliar knot of anxiety rode his midsection. What was Chance encountering in Montana, and Cash discovering in Oregon? Could they be facing worse than this? Obviously the housing project was at a standstill. How in hell would he get it moving again?

Possibly he had one ally, Val LeClair, but would a real estate agent be any asset beyond her sales capabilities? Then again, with her disdain for female fuss and frills, she could be so dedicated to work, she might be a big help. For certain he wasn't in a position to turn his back on any possibility.

Rush looked at the file cabinets, which probably contained the company records. He got up and started for them, then changed his mind. He was tired and out of sorts. Worried. He'd do much better in the morning with perturbing facts and figures than he would tonight.

Switching off lights, he locked the office and drove to the motel. But inside the small room and staring at the array of luggage, another thought disturbed his peace: He couldn't afford to live in a motel for long.

Undressing, he took a shower and crawled into bed, thinking, *Tomorrow will be the first day of the rest of your life.*

The profound concept at first shook him, then offered a strange sort of comfort. He was on his own, and no way was he going to run to his older brothers just because the future looked bleak. Their problems in Oregon and Montana wouldn't be precisely the same as what he was facing in Nevada, but they had them, make no mistake.

He decided he was lucky to have even one ally, and if Val LeClair had only half the strength she projected, she could prove to be a valuable friend.

Yawning, he turned to his side and closed his eyes. Tomorrow was crucial and he was exhausted. In minutes he was sleeping.

Val got home about 1:00 a.m., which was normal for her. The main showroom of the massive Casbah Hotel and Casino had been filled to capacity tonight, also normal. So were the notes from would-be Lotharios delivered backstage. Though she never read them anymore, she knew their messages. *"Please let me meet you, lovely lady." "Please allow an enormous fan the privilege of saying hello, sweet Valentine."*

She never complied with the requests, she never even acknowledged them. She was so sick and tired of the entertainment world, she could barely force herself into her costume and going onstage anymore. Every man she met was gaga over her being a showgirl, and not one of them ever tried to see beneath the glitz and glamour to the woman she really was.

But dancing onstage in outrageous costumes paid fairly well, and her real estate career, which she had hoped would finance her break with show business, had taken a disappointing downswing because of the Saxon Company's troubles. She'd sunk all of her real estate eggs into one basket, a mistake, many agents believed. At the time, about a year ago, working on only one housing project had seemed sensible. Buyers of tract housing appeared during daylight hours, and some agents she knew were busy nearly every evening with clients. She couldn't do that, not if she wanted to keep her job in the Casbah Hotel's showroom, which was necessary until her second career got off the ground.

Throughout the years Valentine LeClair had made good money performing onstage, but most of it had been used to pay for her mother's care in a nursing home. Doris LeClair passed away fourteen months ago, and it was right around that time that Val made the decision to find herself a more stable and normal career. She enrolled in real estate school and passed the Nevada state exam with flying colors. Eager to get started, she shopped around for a brokerage to hang her license. By accident she stumbled across the Saxon Construction Company, which needed an on-site agent, and the job seemed perfect for her particular needs.

She'd worked hard since, and those eighty-seven sales represented a lot of money in terms of her commissions, which she would never realize unless those sales closed, which wouldn't happen if the houses didn't get finished.

Pondering Rush Saxon's startling arrival at the office earlier in the night, Val went through her usual after-show routine. She had already removed her heavy stage makeup before leaving the Casbah, but she always got home keyed-up and relaxed with a cup of hot herbal tea and a piece of cinnamon toast.

Val's home was a pleasant condominium situated on a lovely swath of green grass and evergreen trees. The amenities included an attached garage and several community swimming pools, as well as a superbly equipped workout room which she used often. Dancing was a demanding profession, and while excess weight had never been a problem, keeping herself supple and in top-notch physical condition required time and effort. All in all, her life was filled with activity, so much so that any sudden, unexpected free time felt almost unnatural.

She hadn't really dated anyone in years, though she had good friends she could call for a movie or a dinner out. She was thirty years old and had never been married. Some of the other dancers in the show had wonderful relationships, so she was positive she simply hadn't met the right man.

By the same token, she wasn't looking. But if she ever did, she knew he would not be the careless playboy type. Her idea of Mr. Right didn't require wealth or great looks. She just wanted someone who had both feet on the ground, a reasonable amount of ambition and an affection for the human race, qualities she was beginning to believe were rare indeed among the male gender.

Take Rush Saxon, for instance. Too good-looking, without question. Wealthy and flaunting it. Overly confident. Reckless, perhaps. Probably spoiled rotten and conceited from women tripping over themselves to get his attention. Granted she was forming an opinion on a very brief acquaintanceship, but first impressions were generally quite close to accurate.

Valentine LeClair would not enter that free-for-all. Her only interest in the macho Mr. Saxon was to help him get his project on the road again so she could collect her commissions and quit dancing!

Sipping her tea, Val kicked her shoes off her aching feet. Thirty was hardly ancient, but some of the other performers in the show were under twenty. Most of them were certainly under twenty-five. She was one of the "older" women in the spectacular stage show, and her feet were beginning to feel their age.

A Saxon on the scene was exhilarating, though, regardless of how she personally viewed the man. For several weeks now she had feared the whole project turning into a dead issue. Daily she made calls to her buyers in an attempt to keep them pacified, though she couldn't blame any of them for being concerned and worse, angry. They had put money down on the house they wanted, which was in escrow, thank God, and untouchable. Should the project fail entirely, the buyers would get their money back.

But it would be far, far better for everyone concerned if the buyers got their houses, the Saxon Construction Company got their profits, and she got her sales commissions.

Rush Saxon would see that it all happened, Val assured herself. Why else would he be here? With his money, there was no reason for any other conclusion.

Suddenly anxious for tomorrow, Val brought her cup to the kitchen sink and went to her bedroom. She fell asleep assuring herself that everything was going to work out now. Within weeks—a month at the latest—she should start receiving her commissions as the house sales closed, and soon thereafter she could give her notice of resignation to the Casbah's showroom manager.

It would be a marvelous day for her, one she had been looking forward to for a long, long time.

Two

Arriving at the Saxon office at nine-thirty the next morning, Val was pleased to see Rush's car parked in front. Apparently he really did intend to do something about the company's sad financial condition, which would put everything back on track.

She got out of her car and hurried into the office. Rush was seated at a desk. "Good morning."

He stared, not because she looked different from last night but because she didn't. Instead of jeans, she had on a skirt, but today's blouse wasn't any more exciting than last night's had been. And she still wasn't wearing makeup. What puzzled him was why any woman would deliberately wreak havoc with her most appealing asset, such as Val did with that unbecoming hairdo, particularly when it was such a glorious sun and honey color. How long was it? How would she look with it cascading around her face?

He gave his head a small shake to clear it. "Good morning."

"Hope I haven't kept you waiting." Val laid her purse on her desk.

"Your time is your own," Rush said coolly.

Val stiffened slightly. "Yes, it is, but this project has become very important to me."

"Because of the sales commissions."

Was there disdain in his voice? Val hesitated, decided to overlook what she'd heard and nodded. "Commissions are what I'm working for, and I've earned every one of them, Mr. Saxon." Lord knew that was the truth. She'd sold some of those houses twice and three times to the same buyers, reassuring them repeatedly that the delay in completion was only a temporary setback to a reasonable closing date.

Her formal address tightened Rush's lips, but he decided that venting his bad mood on Val was neither fair nor wise. His tension was caused by worry, after all, not by her tardiness. He'd been sitting at this desk going over records since seven, and if he understood what he'd been reading, this company was on the verge of bankruptcy. The bank account had a pitiable balance, and there was a stack of unpaid bills thick enough to choke an elephant.

It would have cheered him up, he realized, if Val LeClair had come flouncing in wearing something sexy, or at least feminine. He'd like to rid her hair of that tortuous style, just unpin it and set it free, and then brazenly suggest that she buy herself a tube of lipstick and use it.

Disgusted with such inane thoughts when the devil himself seemed to be nipping at his heels, Rush threw down his pen and got up from his chair to stretch his back.

Val sat at her desk and opened her purse for her eyeglass case. Watching Rush's gyrations to remove his kinks, she extracted the glasses and put them on. Aware of the aroma of coffee, she got up for a cup.

"I made that over two hours ago," Rush cautioned. "It's probably bitter."

"I only want a sip, but thanks for the warning." The coffeemaker was sitting on top of a file cabinet, and she turned her back to pour some in a disposable cup. She glanced behind her. "Would you like a refill?"

"No, thanks."

Val carried her cup back to her desk and sat down. Saxon looked crisply handsome though harried this morning, again wearing expensive slacks and that diamond-studded watch. She couldn't elude acknowledging his good looks, but she could and would keep her admiration completely private.

"Do you have any questions this morning?" she asked.

There were so many questions doing battle in Rush's brain, he didn't know where to start. Leaning forward slightly, he tapped the checkbook. "Are you aware of the small balance in this account?"

"Only from hearsay."

"Do you have any idea where I might locate Dirk Johnson?"

"There must be an address and a phone number in his personnel file."

"I checked that. The telephone number listed in his file has been disconnected."

"Then he must have moved," Val murmured. A strange premonition was gathering in the pit of her stomach, though she was afraid to allow it to develop. She cleared her throat. "If I may ask, why do you feel it imperative to talk to Dirk?"

Rush shoved his hands into his pants pockets and walked to a front window. The sun outside was so glaringly bright, it hurt his eyes to look at the shimmering asphalt and desert landscaping. He didn't like admitting confusion to anyone, particularly a woman he barely knew, but somehow he had to start clawing his way out of this mess.

"Because I don't know where to start," he finally said in a gruff tone. "I thought he might have some ideas."

Val sat very still, although an urge to pin him down with a barrage of questions was almost unbearable. That premonition was gaining distinction. Her mind raced from possibility to possibility. They all evolved into one clear, concise thought: With an influx of capital, this company wouldn't have any problems, with or without Dirk Johnson.

She took a sip of coffee, barely noticing the bitter taste. Her future was teetering again, hanging by a very weak thread. "Mr. Saxon, uh, Rush, are you planning to give—or loan—this company the money it needs?"

He turned and after staring a moment, barked out a cynical laugh. "Forget that notion, honey. I haven't got a dime to give—or loan—to anyone."

Her expression registered complete shock. "But your family...?"

"Is broke."

"Broke," she repeated tonelessly.

"Crashed, busted, without a sou."

Val's shoulders slumped as she whispered, "Ohmygod."

"Yes, ohmygod," Rush agreed dryly.

"But... what can you do? I mean, what can *we* do? My sales. The project. The buyers." Val knew she was babbling, but couldn't seem to stop herself. "I've been talking the buyers into staying with their purchase offers... promising that the houses would be finished very soon now."

Sighing, Rush returned to his desk. "I don't know what to tell you. There's no money, it's that simple." He scowled down at the checkbook. "Or that complex. I thought if I could talk to Dirk, he might have some suggestions." He glanced over to Val. "What sort of guy is he?"

Val shook her head disgustedly. "Dirk looks out for Dirk. If you want the truth, I never cared for him. Saxon Springs should have been completed months ago, but he shut down the job again and again for any trumped-up excuse. Construction workers will work on weekends and even holidays, Rush, but not if the project manager doesn't give two hoots whether they work or not. I saw Dirk on the site drinking beer with the men more than once, which is no way to run a tight ship."

Stunned, Rush sat back. He'd been thinking of Johnson as his last hope. Familiar with the construction business and this particular project, the man could have been a great deal of help.

Apparently not. So his situation was no money and no knowledgeable advice. And a bunch of unpaid bills and a saleswoman who looked ready to collapse because her commissions were getting farther out of reach by the minute.

He suddenly yearned for a cigarette, which he'd given up three years before. He wished for a *carton* of cigarettes, and a bottle of whiskey, though he'd never been a drinking man.

There were ledgers, the checkbook and financial statements strewn all over his desk. Rush's gaze fell on a letter from a C.P.A. firm, obviously the company's accountants.

"Maybe I should talk to someone at Bernstein and Callahan." He saw the signature on the letter. "Lois Markham. Do you know her?"

"No," Val said in a husky, unsteady voice. The worst was happening, the project was dissolving before her very eyes, and it was too much to grasp. Months of hard work and all of her plans, disappearing, and there wasn't anything she could do to prevent it from happening.

The content of Rush's remark and question registered. Val lifted her eyes as a small hope sprouted. "You're not giving up?"

A frown creased Rush's forehead. "Do you think I should?"

"No! I mean, not yet, anyway. Talking to the accountant is probably a good idea. And maybe you should see the project. It's only about a half mile from here. I could drive you over..."

"Just a minute." Rush picked up the phone and punched out the number on the C.P.A.'s letterhead. "Lois Markham, please," he said when the firm's receptionist answered.

In a few minutes he had arranged an appointment with Ms. Markham. He put down the phone and spoke to Val. "She'll see me at three this afternoon. If you've got the time right now, I'd like to inspect the project."

Nodding, Val removed her glasses and put them away. She was standing when a pickup drove up out front and stopped. Two men got out.

"Do you know them?" Rush asked. The men were obviously laborers, dressed in cutoff jeans and sleeveless T-shirts.

Val sighed. "They're carpenters, Rush. Probably here to pick up a paycheck."

Rush stood up as the two men walked in. They were burly fellows, with darkly tanned, weathered skin and long hair tied back behind their heads. They looked from Val to Rush and back to her again. "Hi, Val."

"Hello."

Rush moved around the desk and offered his hand. "I'm Rush Saxon."

The men looked at each other, then took turns shaking Rush's hand, announcing their names while they did it.

"Jim Logan."

"Alex Robertson."

"What can I do for you?" Rush asked.

"Uh . . . we got some pay coming, Mr. Saxon," Jim, the taller man, said. "We turned in our time five days ago and need the money."

"Can you give me until tomorrow morning to get the checks ready? I only got here last night, and I'm trying to make sense of a pretty bad mess."

The men shifted their weight and again looked at each other. Jim finally nodded. "Guess one more day'll be all right. But we need our pay, Mr. Saxon. Will it be ready tomorrow morning for sure?"

"You can count on it," Rush promised.

"Are you working at the Springs today?" Val questioned.

"We're there," Jim replied. "Well, see you in the morning."

The men filed out, and the atmosphere in the office was suddenly taut with silence. Rush raked his hair. Val's eyes moved to him, containing a question. *Where will you get the money?* He shook his head. "I don't know. Come on, let's drive to the site."

They locked up and got into Val's car, which felt like an oven. Quickly she started the engine and turned on the air conditioner.

"How hot is it?" Rush asked.

"Around a hundred degrees. It's supposed to reach one-ten today." Val backed up the car to turn around. "You're not accustomed to this kind of heat."

"It was great last night."

"Summer nights are perfect, but daytime temperatures are sizzling during July and August. You'll get used to it." *If you're here that long.* Val drove with an ache in her stomach. It all seemed so hopeless, and such an enormous waste. How could Rush make things right without money? How could anyone?

But she would do anything she could to help him try. "The site is just ahead," she announced.

Rush peered into the distance. The houses were in various stages of construction, and some of them looked finished. He counted. "About a dozen of them are close to completion, apparently."

"Fourteen, to be exact. What's missing are kitchen appliances and some finish carpentry. And carpet," she added after a second.

"Costly items." Rush frowned at the sight of five exquisitely finished houses, adorned with flags and banners and surrounded by mature landscaping, an island of greenery within the otherwise dusty construction site. "What are those?"

"The models. I don't know how familiar you are with development routines, but normally a developer puts up the models very quickly so prospective buyers can see the finished product. They're already sold, of course, but the buyers are fully aware that the models are virtually the last sales to close in a project.''

"Wait a minute. You mean those five houses are completely finished and sold, and we can't close the sales until the other houses are finished?''

Val pulled over to the curb in front of the models. "That's normal procedure.''

"But who makes that decision? I mean, is it a law or something?''

"A law? A real estate regulation, you mean? Why no, not that I know of. It's just common practice. Without models, a project would sell out very slowly.''

"But you said we're seventy-nine percent sold-out.''

"That's true.'' She studied the handsome man in her passenger seat. "What are you thinking?''

Rush reached for the door handle. "I'm thinking of getting the sales on those models closed as fast as possible. Come on. Show me the interiors.''

The models were not only finished right down to the appliances and carpeting, but they were furnished and beautifully decorated. "Who owns this furniture?''

"You do.''

"I don't believe this,'' Rush mumbled as he walked through the five houses. Each was decorated differently, imaginatively, and there was an incredible amount of good furniture, knickknacks, paintings and pictures on the walls, bedspreads on the beds, and even towels in the bathrooms.

He stopped in the last model to thoughtfully rub his mouth. "How does a sale close in Nevada?''

"Down payments are in escrow with a title company. They're simply awaiting word to proceed with the paperwork.'' Val's heart was beating hard and fast. Closing the sales on the models was maybe premature—there were still twenty-three unfinished houses to sell—but the company would receive enough money from those closings to keep going. How had she overlooked that solution?

Rush was still thinking. "With the money from these closings, we could push the carpenters on those other fourteen houses. Val, it just might work."

Her excitement was mounting. "It *will* work, Rush."

He grinned, the first she'd seen, and her heart took a sudden flip in her chest. "All I have to do now is figure out how to pay Jim and Alex in the morning."

"There'll be others after money," Val reminded on a cautioning note.

But Rush was on a roll and feeling rather incautious. "How long do you think it will take the title company to close?"

"At least two weeks."

"Then we just have to find a way to survive for two weeks." Elated, Rush grabbed Val in a big hug. It wasn't intended as a pass, but he was suddenly aware of her body against his. As tall as she was, she felt small in his arms, and he was surprised by her firmness.

An unexpected thrill rocketed through Val. The hug had come without warning. She didn't want to get huffy about it, not when it meant nothing to Rush beyond an expression of relief. But he felt much too good against her, and his scent was making her dizzy.

She placed her hands on his chest and pushed gently. Rush took a backward step. His grin had vanished, replaced by a slightly perplexed look. "Sorry."

She shaped a weak smile. "Forget it." Striving for composure, she adjusted the strap of her bag on her shoulder. "Let's go back to the office so I can make some calls."

"Right," Rush agreed. Following her out, however, he had to question his strong reaction to Val. She had a fantastic body, almost hard in its firmness. Her breasts were full and pillow-soft, though, and he could still feel their imprint on his chest.

She wasn't the kind of woman he was normally drawn to. He liked flash and dash, women who made the most of what nature had given them, women with style and a flair for the dramatic. Val smelled like spring flowers, probably soap, and if there was any drama in her personality, he couldn't see it.

And yet he'd wanted her immediately, the second he'd brought her close in that impulsive hug.

In the car he gave her a sideways glance. She was sitting almost primly, probably already light-years away from that disturbing hug. Obviously it hadn't affected her, not when her only reaction had been to push him away.

Rush was wrong in his assessment of Val's reaction. She couldn't stop thinking about it, in fact. It was only a simple hug, she kept telling herself while she drove, nothing to get starry-eyed about. Rush Saxon might have come up with a startlingly brilliant idea to prolong the company's life today, but one great idea didn't make him the ideal man.

He wasn't right for her, no more than she was right for him. And heaven knew she wasn't receptive to playing around just for the fun of it. She'd been down that road before, and it always came to a painful dead end.

Her goals now were those of a mature woman. She wanted stability and an income that didn't depend on how long she could compete with the myriad of young dancers out there. Someday the right man might come along, but she wasn't at all unhappy living alone.

Val parked next to Rush's rental car, the sight of which made him frown. He couldn't keep paying a daily rate for a car, and he had to find somewhere else to sleep besides that motel room.

The hug became buried beneath his many problems. He got out of Val's car and walked around the front of it. His skin felt scorched from the blazing sun.

"Need any help with the title companies?" he asked.

"I don't think so. Why?"

"I'm going to leave for a while. Got a few things that need doing."

"Fine, no problem." Val watched him approach his own car with the keys in his hand.

He stopped before getting in. "Maybe you know of something to rent for a reasonable price?"

"Housing?"

"I'm in a motel right now."

Val bit her lip. Her involvement in real estate didn't include rental properties, but one of the condos in her complex was for rent by its owner, Larry Caldwell, who was planning a three-month tour of Europe. Mostly Larry wanted someone substantial and reliable to live in his place for security reasons, and Val suspected he wouldn't demand a high rent. But did she want Rush Saxon living that close to her?

She suddenly felt petty. Her condo complex was huge and Larry's unit was well away from hers. It would be perfect for Rush, as it was completely furnished and available in mere days.

"Uh...I'm not positive it's still open, but..." Words tumbling out, Val related what she knew about Larry's unit. "He's probably at home, as he's getting ready for his trip." She recited the address. "You might stop and talk to him. It would probably help to mention you know me."

Rush nodded eagerly. "Sounds great, Val. Thanks." He opened the door of his car. "See you later."

She unlocked the office and went inside frowning. Her and Rush Saxon's lives were becoming much too intertwined, but how could she not have told him about Larry's condo when he was living in a motel?

It didn't occur to her until she was seated at her desk and digging out her reading glasses that she hadn't told Rush about Larry's address being only digits away from her own. She sighed, wondering why fate seemed so intent on putting her in uneasy situations. It hadn't, not until recently. Not until Rush Saxon arrived in Las Vegas.

Val had all five closings on line by four that afternoon. She had made numerous phone calls to the buyers and their respective title companies, gone out briefly for a bite of lunch, answered the phone at least a dozen times, fielded the prying questions of three bill collectors who appeared in person and ultimately realized that she'd acted as receptionist for the Saxon Construction Company all day.

Sitting back, Val mulled her situation over. Other than an occasional rehearsal at the Casbah, her days were her own. Simply selling a house wasn't enough in this case, though few sales were ever simple, she was beginning to comprehend from conversations with longtime agents. "Never spend your commission before the check is in your hand" was advice she heard over and over again. "A hundred things can go wrong and kill the deal. I had one last month that looked absolutely certain to close, and ten minutes before the final papers were signed, the buyer had a fatal heart attack. End of sale."

Being relatively new to the business had its drawbacks, Val knew. She was learning, though, and doing so the hard way. Even if it took grit and tenacity and most of her time to baby-sit those sales into closing, didn't it make sense to comply?

She dreamed of a future without a connection to the Casbah, when her only obligations would be to real estate clients. Ultimately she would have to work for a broker. A developer could hire an agent without going through a broker, which was her arrangement with the Saxon Company. Without a broker, however, she couldn't take any listings on other properties.

Until recently, she had believed her arrangement to be perfect for her needs. Whether it proved profitable or a bust depended on Rush. If he made a go of the business, she had made the right decision. If not . . . ?

Sighing, Val got up from the desk and walked to a front window. Where was he? Had he kept his appointment with the accountant? She wanted to tell him about the headway she'd made with the title companies, but she wasn't keen on hanging around indefinitely.

Staring out the window at the baking landscape beyond the air-conditioned office, Val thought again of that hug between her and Rush. It was a small incident, trivial, actually, but it kept appearing and reappearing in her mind. Rush Saxon was a sexy guy, potent, and it had been a long time since she'd made love with any man. That's probably all her giddy reaction to Rush's embrace meant, just a reminder of her own abstinence.

But reminders that made her restless were annoying and unwanted. She deliberately went without makeup and stylish clothes during the day to discourage the kind of response she got from men at night at the Casbah. Rush couldn't possibly find her attractive in her all-business disguise.

She laughed shortly, slicing the silence of the office. "Disguise" was maybe melodramatic, but she liked nice clothes and perfume as well as the next woman, and she possessed both. She knew more about makeup than most women, and how to arrange her hair into a sensual tangle that made men's fingers itch to touch it. The proof of that observation was in the notes scrawled on cocktail napkins and bits of paper she received after many of her performances.

But that was what she wanted to get away from. Many people she knew had no idea that she danced on the Strip, Larry Caldwell, for instance, thank God. Rush wouldn't learn anything about "Valentine" from Larry, because to the people living in her condo complex, she was merely Val LeClair.

At a quarter to five, Val cleared her desk and got her purse. She was ready to leave when she spotted a car driving in. It was far from new, one of those squat little foreign jobs without a top, and her first thought was "Good Lord, that guy must be cooking!"

Then she saw the driver was Rush, and her mouth dropped open. He got out grinning and came in. "What do you think of the wheels?"

"Are you roasted clear through?" she asked dryly.

"The salesman offered me a good deal and I couldn't pass it up."

"Probably couldn't sell it to anyone else in this heat."

"Could be, but I needed something inexpensive. I was driving a rental car, you know. By the way, I made a deal with Larry Caldwell. I'll be moving in on Saturday. Thanks for the tip."

Val was noticing something odd: Rush wasn't wearing his watch. He walked to his desk. "I made a deposit at the bank," he said while fishing a slip of paper from his shirt pocket. Val watched him make a notation in the checkbook. "Now I can pay Jim and Alex in the morning."

She knew then that he'd hocked his watch. Her heart seemed suddenly lodged in her throat. "Did you see the accountant?" she asked in a small voice.

"Sure did. Lois waltzed me through some figures, Val, and when the sales on those models close, this company will be solvent." He grinned. "*Reasonably* solvent."

"You've been . . . busy," she said quietly.

"Running around like a chicken without a head," Rush said cheerfully. "Hey, how about having dinner with me tonight?"

"Uh . . . no. I can't. I talked to the buyers and the title companies, and everything's underway for the closings on the models."

"Fantastic! Are you sure you can't join me for dinner? We should celebrate after accomplishing so much today."

"Thanks, but I really can't."

"Got a date?" Rush teased.

"Yes," she lied. Val picked up her purse. "I won't be here tomorrow, but I can give you my home phone number in case you need to talk to me."

Rush nodded. "Great, thanks."

Val took out her business card and wrote her home number on it. "I'm glad things turned out so well for you today."

"The day turned out well for both of us, Val. You'll be receiving some nice commission checks from those closings." Rush took the business card from her hand, and Val's gaze lit on his bare left wrist. Rush smiled. "I'll get my watch back someday. Don't let it bother you."

"You're serious about getting this company on course, aren't you?" she said.

"Deadly serious, Val. Will you help me?"

"I'll do anything I can."

"Thanks, I really appreciate it."

Val wondered during the drive home if she hadn't misjudged Rush's character. Surely a careless individual wouldn't have done what he had today.

She sighed, because she was beginning to really like Rush Saxon, and it felt dangerous and slightly traitorous to her own goals to do so.

Three

———

Rush had his celebration dinner, though it was of modest cost and solitary. He indulged in one scotch before eating and let his mind wander while he sipped it.

He had never come close to a business deal before, and yet he had managed something today that had seemed utterly impossible only this morning: find a way to keep the company afloat until he could figure out the next step.

There was an unfamiliar zing of excitement in his system, coming from a source he had little experience with: pride in himself. Oh, there had been plenty of prideful moments in his thirty years, but they'd been derived from things like winning a tennis match with a skilled opponent, or being the life of a party, where everyone laughed at his wit, or catching a beautiful woman after an exhilarating chase. Never anything to do with basic human needs, he realized over his scotch. Other people worked for a living, the Saxons did not.

But the Saxons were working now, and actually accomplishing something on his own was a brand-new high for Rush. He thought of his grandfather, and wondered why the old gentleman had never tried to instill any of his own ambition into his grandsons. Clearly the eldest Saxon had given too much, atoning for the loss of his grandsons' mother and father with material possessions. With money. Never cautioning them to spend more wisely. Never suggesting they put their educations to some use.

It was damned odd, Rush thought. Odd that the money should suddenly be gone. Odd that no one had said, "Hey, boys, if you don't slow down, there won't be anything left." Surely Granddad and his lawyer, Robert Teale, had to have seen the handwriting on the wall long before the final crash.

"Odd," Rush murmured, taking a small swallow from his glass. He grinned to himself about the day again, thinking of Val. She was a fine woman, willing to do what she could to help. Of course, she was undoubtedly motivated by her threatened commissions, but still, how many women that he knew would be so generous with their time?

It was a damned shame that she had so little style. Would she feel insulted if he offered to take her shopping? Dressing her long, fabulous body would be a pleasure. Something slinky and softly draped, he could almost picture it. And he knew exactly how he'd like to see her hair, all tumbled and curled around her face. Makeup, of course, all of the gunk and goo that could change an ordinary-looking woman into a siren.

She had incredible eyes, a striking liquid-brown, and long lashes, and the fullness of her lips would be irresistible with subtle color delineating their marvelous shape.

Rush suddenly frowned into his drink. Speaking of fullness, who would ever suspect the lush, ripe breasts under those awful blouses Val wore? Was she deliberately disguising her femaleness? Why would she do that? Any woman should be proud of a body like Val's.

He was drawn to Val LeClair, willingly or not, he finally had to admit. Drawn to her body, if nothing else. He liked her height, and the way she walked with her back straight and her head high. There was an unusual gracefulness in her walk. The truth was, the woman would be a knockout with a little effort. Didn't she know that?

Scowling slightly, Rush finished off his drink and gestured to the waiter: He was ready to order dinner.

There were a lot of temptations for a single man in Las Vegas. Gambling, of course, any form of gambling anyone could want. And glamorous shows featuring beautiful, exciting women and extremely talented musicians. Comedians, magicians, singers, dancers, each hotel-casino touted its stage show as the best, the biggest, the most spectacular.

He didn't have money to waste, but he had an evening to kill, and Rush drove his tiny MG down the Strip to soak up the atmosphere. His progress was kept slow by the heavy traffic, but he loved the warm night air and enjoyed the drive.

Peering at the massive signs in front of each hotel-casino, he read the attractions. There were two famous singers in town. He'd like to see both shows, but figured he'd better watch his dollars very closely for a while. If the company moved along as he hoped, there'd be money for stage shows later on.

He drove past the Casbah and read its huge sign: Gala Stage Show, Featuring The Beautiful Dancer, Valentine!

Rush racked his brain, but he was positive he'd never heard of a performer named Valentine. Maybe he'd see the Casbah's show, too, he decided. When he felt comfortable about spending money on entertainment, of course.

Shifting the MG into first, Rush made a left turn and got away from the Strip. The hour was late, and he figured he wouldn't have any trouble sleeping now. He headed for his motel and bed.

Val took care of a lengthy list of errands the next day, which included grocery shopping, a stop at the dry cleaners and some banking. When she wasn't working at one job or the other, she lived in shorts and sandals in this hot climate, and today her shorts were white, her T-shirt blue and her sandals natural leather.

She was wearing light makeup and her hair was only slightly restrained, drawn back from her face with combs. This was how she normally looked; this was the genuine Valentine Marie LeClair. Neither the glamorous woman on stage nor the stodgy real estate agent persona came close to her true self. Both were an act, she felt, and someday she wanted to meet a man who liked shorts and sneakers, casual food and good books, as she did, a man who wasn't impressed because she performed onstage, nor gave two hoots that she dressed down and plainly for real estate clients.

Rush Saxon wasn't him, she reminded herself again while carrying her groceries into her condo. And that one hug was all she would ever allow between them. If that simple gesture bothered her so much, imagine what a real clinch with Rush would do to her.

No, thanks, she thought, disgusted that she had awakened in the night—close to dawn, actually—to think about that accursed hug again.

Her message machine was blinking, so she put down the groceries on the kitchen counter and poked the Play button. Rush's voice filled the room. "Hi, Val. Sorry to bother you at home, but I had a call from the *Review-Journal.* What's your opinion on the company doing some newspaper advertising on the project at this point? Call me. I'll be at the office most of the day."

There were two other messages, which Val made note of on the pad next to the phone. But it was Rush's that disturbed her. Not that his question was out of line. Advertising should be a joint decision between owner and Realtor, but just the sound of his voice was unsettling.

It was silly, of course, nothing but female foolishness, which she thought she was beyond. Angry at herself, she grabbed the phone and punched out the office number.

"Hello," Rush said. "Saxon Construction Company."

Val cleared her throat. "This is Val. There's a message on my machine..."

"Oh, great. Val, what do you think about doing some advertising right now?"

"Well...it's costly, Rush. Ordinarily I would recommend keeping a project before the public, but you'll have to decide in this case."

"But if money wasn't a consideration, you would vote yes."

"Definitely. There are still twenty-three houses to move, and when the models are gone, those last units could be difficult to sell."

"Can we use the models up to their closing dates?"

"I don't see why not. The buyers are completely aware of those houses' status. They bought them because they *are* models, Rush, and decorated so nicely. A lot of people can't visualize how a house will look with wallpaper and decorator touches. I've heard from Realtors in the business longer than myself that the models are often the first sales in a project."

"Even though they sell for more money."

"That's right."

"All right, fine. I was thinking of something else, Val. You've probably been holding open houses on the models, right?"

"Every weekend."

"Can we do that this weekend?"

"Certainly."

"Great. That's what I'm going to put in the ad. It'll come out in Saturday morning's paper if I call the guy back right now. Talk to you later, and thanks for your input."

"Anytime," Val murmured.

A few minutes later, while she was placing milk and eggs in the refrigerator, her front doorbell chimed. "Coming," she called, and wound through the condo to open the door.

Larry Caldwell was standing on her stoop. "Oh, hello, Larry."

"Hello, Val. Could I talk to you for a minute?"

"Sure. Come on in." People didn't keep visitors on their front stoop in hundred-degree weather, not unless they didn't care if the heat poured through the open door and defeated the air-conditioning.

Larry stepped inside. He was a small, fussy man, around fifty, Val believed, a man who always said hello when he passed by and usually invited his neighbors in for a drink over the Christmas holidays. His condo was more expensively appointed than Val's, though its floor plan was similar.

"Can I get you something cold to drink?" Val inquired.

"No, but thank you. I merely wanted to discuss Mr. Saxon with you."

"Rush Saxon, yes. He told me you made a rental agreement with him."

"That's correct, but I got to thinking about it. He said he knew you, and he has an extremely charming nature. I hope I didn't rush into that agreement too quickly."

Val wasn't completely easy about vouching for Rush, but she couldn't bring herself to undermine his agreement with Larry. "He's the owner of Saxon Construction Company, Larry, which is the company behind the Saxon Springs project. Did he tell you?"

"Yes, he did. But he's very new to the area, and I guess I just need to hear your opinion of him, Val. Hope you don't mind."

"Well...I haven't known him long, Larry. But so far I feel he's honest and determined to make something out of a company that's had some difficult problems."

"Financial problems?"

"Among others, yes."

"Oh, dear," Larry murmured worriedly. "I have some very valuable possessions in my condo, Val."

"I know you do. I never would have given him your name if I'd thought for a minute he wouldn't take care of your possessions. Rush is from a wealthy family, Larry. I suspect he's completely familiar with valuable possessions."

Larry's eyes lit up. "He didn't tell me that."

"Well, I'm not sure he wants people to know every detail of his background."

"And you trust him?"

Val laughed. "I'd better trust him. I've sold dozens of his houses and hope to collect every one of my commissions."

"That's right! I forgot about your selling real estate. How remiss of me! You're working for Mr. Saxon. Well, that certainly throws a different light on the matter. I feel much better about it. Much."

"Are you all ready to leave on your trip?" Val asked as Larry started for the door.

"Almost."

Val opened the door. "If I don't see you before you leave, have a wonderful time."

Larry nodded. "I'm sure I will. I love to travel."

After goodbyes, Val closed the door and leaned her back against it. If Rush didn't take care of Larry's condo, the burden of responsibility was going to land on her. Damn! Why had she even told him about it? She didn't want him living so close, petty or not, and now this.

What's more, hadn't Rush distinctly said "we" in regard to the open house this weekend? He was planning to be there with her, all weekend. Just how would she deal with that?

Val wearily pushed away from the door and returned to the kitchen and her groceries. This was going to be a busy, complicated weekend, Rush moving into her condo complex, then the two of them tending to the models. She had shows on Friday and Saturday nights, although the Casbah's showroom was traditionally dark on Sundays and Mondays.

But if she'd had any ideas about avoiding Rush Saxon, she may as well forget them. He was slithering deeper into her life by the hour.

Rush was thrilled to haul his things into Larry's spacious unit early Saturday morning, three trips from motel to condo complex with the tiny MG loaded to the max each time. He'd come in time for Larry to give him a set of keys before leaving for the airport. They shook hands and agreed to talk on the phone whenever Larry managed to call. And since Rush could see that Larry was a little nervous about putting his home in a stranger's hands, he tried to reassure him.

"Don't worry about your place, Larry. I guarantee that it will be exactly the same when you get back from Europe."

"Well...that's about what Val told me. She's a good neighbor, Rush, and I trust her judgment."

Rush casually raised an eyebrow. "Expect she is." He looked out the window at the multitude of similar condominiums, all of them white with royal blue window awnings. "I forgot the number of her unit."

"Four-fourteen," replied Larry. "It's just around that wide curve in the sidewalk and about halfway to the front gate."

Rush nodded. "Right. Four-fourteen. I won't forget it again. Well, have a great trip, Larry." He stuck out his hand, which the smaller man clasped in another slightly sweaty handshake. "Enjoy yourself."

"I always rent my home during extended trips, and I always worry," Larry admitted. "For the first few days, anyway."

They laughed together and walked to the door. When Larry was gone, Rush breathed a sigh of relief and took a stroll through the apartment that would be his home for the next three months.

He would be staying in the guest room, which was stunningly decorated in black and white. Rush suspected the entire condo was professionally decorated. Either that or Larry was an exceptionally talented fellow.

He unpacked every suitcase, grimacing at the wrinkles in his good clothes. But he hung them on padded hangers, hoping the wrinkles would hang out. Sending everything to the cleaners would have been his first impulse a short time ago; right now he didn't have that much extra cash.

He peered into the almost empty refrigerator and decided to use some of his cash for food. Preparing his own meals would save a whale of a lot of money. He glanced at his watch and figured he had plenty of time to do some grocery shopping. The open house at the models was set to start at ten, which was still two hours away.

Whistling through his teeth, Rush left Larry's condo and went outside to his car. He stopped to grin: For certain he wasn't going to get a whole lot of groceries in the MG.

Val felt an almost irrepressible urge to primp for the open house. She looked longingly at a favorite dress, a multicolored gauze that draped over her lanky figure in a pleasing fashion. Rush would be surprised if she appeared in that kind of dress, and it might be interesting to see his reaction.

Grimly Val reached for a plain gray shirtwaist. Before real estate, she had dressed up the gray with a wide red belt, red shoes and brightly colored jewelry. Today she used the matching fabric belt, no jewelry at all and slipped on a pair of white midheel pumps. Plain fare. *Uninteresting* fare.

She brushed her hair back and pinned it into a dull knot. Her face was clean and shiny, a little too shiny, so she brought down its sheen with a light dusting of powder.

Giving herself fifteen minutes for the drive to the Saxon Springs project, she parked to one side of the models right on the stroke of ten.

Rush had preceded her, she saw by his car. She went into the first unit, whose garage had been converted into a temporary sales office. Rush got up from the desk. "Good morning."

Val stared and then deliberately averted her gaze from his startling good looks. "Good morning, Rush. Any early activity?"

"The ad said ten."

She still couldn't look at him. "Yes, but sometimes there are early birds waiting for the doors to open."

"No sign of anyone yet."

"I see you made a pot of coffee. Good." Val went over to the pot and stack of disposable cups. "Did you get settled in Larry's condo?" she asked while filling a cup.

Rush smiled. "Sure did. By the way, he called you a good neighbor."

Val flushed slightly. "Didn't I tell you I live in the same complex?"

"Maybe you did," he said generously, eyeing her outfit with inner disapproval. It was as bland as breakfast mush. No makeup again, and that same unbecoming hairstyle. He'd hoped she would dress up for the open house, knock his socks off with some dramatic outfit, swingy, curled hair and lots of eye shadow.

She looked like an old-maid schoolteacher and didn't have to. That's what bothered him. She didn't have to go around as drab and colorless as a gray mouse. With her figure and features, she could compete with the most stunning women in the city.

He sat down, annoyed to bad manners by her lack of self-interest. Val went to the second desk and pulled out the chair. Seated, she couldn't resist looking at him one second longer. Her heart nearly stopped. Rush was wearing a knockout suit constructed of some creamy fabric that fit like a dream. His shirt was the same color, and his silk tie just slightly darker. He was so handsome, it actually hurt to look at him, and she felt like she was wearing a mop rag and should be banished from his illustrious presence.

What's more, she could smell him across the six feet separating the two desks, and whatever incredible scent was wafting from his elegant body shouldn't be allowed in mixed company.

She turned her head and sipped hot coffee and wished she were dead, or at least invisible. Anyone walking through that door would instantly think of *Beauty and the Beast*, and she didn't have to puzzle over it to figure out which of them fit which label.

"So," Rush said. "You look a little tired this morning. Did you have a late night?"

"No later than normal," she grumbled.

She must have a lover, Rush thought, and was immediately surprised by the pang of jealousy he felt. Was her lover as colorless as she was?

He wanted to dig into her personal life, to ask her age, why she dressed the way she did, and who her boyfriend was.

"I talked to the title companies again yesterday afternoon," Val said then. "The paperwork is moving along on those closings."

"Wonderful," Rush murmured absently, adding after a moment, "The sooner the better."

"That's what I told them. The buyers all agree, as well, so as soon as the title companies do their part..." She stopped, wondering why on earth she was babbling again. "Well, you get my drift."

"So this is an open house," Rush commented after a rather uncomfortable stretch of silence.

"It will be as soon as some looky-loos come along."

"Looky-loos? Prospective buyers?"

"Statistically, a very small percentage of lookers are actually interested in buying. Most of them use open houses as entertainment."

"You're kidding."

Val shrugged. "You get used to it."

"But how could anyone have so little to do that they would get a bang out of looking at houses they don't even want?"

"Oh, they probably want them. These are nice houses. But not everyone can afford these prices. You'll learn to weed out the looky-loos from the genuine article. If you do this very much, that is."

Rush set his jaw. "I intend to do it until every one of these houses is sold."

Val smiled. "I thought that was my job."

"Well, it is, but…" An idea occurred to him. "Val, I have no intention of infringing on your commissions."

Her eyes widened. "I didn't mean to imply you did. I'm sorry if my remark gave you that impression."

Rush got to his feet. "I'm going to unlock the other models."

"Good idea," Val murmured, realizing that she should have done that the minute she got here. Rush had muddled her thinking, him and his dashing suit and sexy scent. Disgruntled, she decided she didn't like his suit or his scent. Men who dressed as he did weren't to be trusted. He really must have been something when he had all the money in the world to throw around. What a blow it must have been to his almighty ego finding himself broke.

In the next heartbeat Val called herself sour grapes and a few less flattering names. She had clothes in her closet just as stunning as Rush's suit and tie. She hadn't had to come here looking like a scarecrow.

All right, fine, she argued. What do you want, him writing stupid notes like those morons in the Casbah showroom? *"Oh, Valentine. Your legs are to die for." "Sweetheart, give me the chance to make you happy. I've got all the right equipment."*

It made her sick. Small wonder she'd gone so far in the opposite direction in her daytime career. Would she ever reach the point where a happy medium was all she tried for?

Where she could meet new men without dressing to scare them off?

She'd been leered at, ogled, lusted after and whistled at much too long, for twelve years, in fact, since she was eighteen years old. Drooling men had started making her feel ill several years ago.

But Rush Saxon hadn't drooled, nor would he ever drool. Not if she kept walking around looking like something the cat wouldn't drag in.

Val put her cheek in her hand, muttering, "Oh, damn." She was torn and didn't want to be. Before Rush everything was fine. Her personal life, if not her business, was in good order. Now she was wondering if she was doing anything right.

A car pulled up in front. Val dropped her hand. The first visitors to the open house had arrived. She eyeballed their car and their clothing, and quickly decided they had potential.

She was waiting at the door with a cheerful smile when they came in. "Good morning. Welcome to Saxon Springs."

Four

At four o'clock Val locked the outside door of the models' sales office with a groan of relief. She was exhausted. By actual count, forty-six groups of people—mostly couples—had trooped through the houses and picked up brochures on the project. Val had smiled and repeated the same information so many times, her head ached. But today's open house had been a rousing success; she had three signed Offer to Purchase forms with earnest money checks.

The headache was for real. Wearily Val plopped down at her desk and dug through her purse for some aspirin. Rush had driven off about an hour ago, and Val figured he was gone for the day. What she needed to do was go home, eat a light supper and lie down for a few hours before heading for the Casbah, as she felt utterly drained, and performing onstage demanded a high energy level.

She swallowed the aspirin with water and then closed her eyes and massaged the tension in her temples with her fingertips. Three purchase offers in one day was gratifying, but it would be surprising if all three held up. One out of three was a more realistic hope, which would still make the day profitable for both her and Rush.

Tomorrow would be easier, Val knew, as she wouldn't be concerned about a show at the end of the day. Sighing, she began pulling the pins from her hair. It felt good to release that knot, and to rub her scalp and the back of her neck.

Feeling a little looser, she undid the two top buttons on her dress and seemed able to breathe more freely. There were only a few things left to do before she went home, make sure all of the models were locked, and tidy up in here.

Standing, she did a few long stretches to limber her back, then she fell forward from the waist and let her upper body limply dangle. It was a relaxing exercise, one of the few she truly enjoyed. Leaning over in that position, her hair nearly touched the floor. She straightened up and flipped it back, and nearly fainted when she saw Rush standing at the glass door watching her.

Embarrassed, she hurried over to the door to unlock it. "Don't you have your key?"

Rush wore a puzzled, curious expression. "I left it on the desk." He couldn't stop staring. With her hair down and her face flushed, Val looked ten years younger. His tongue got the better of him. "You should wear your hair down like this. It looks great."

Val pushed it back from her face, a nervous gesture. "It would be in the way."

"I wondered how long it was."

"Now you know," she said flatly, though her heart was beating ridiculously fast. In a way she felt betrayed, spied on. She'd thought she was alone, or she never would have let go so completely. "I thought you'd left for the day."

"I took a drive around the project is all."

"You might have told me."

"You were talking to some clients," Rush pointed out. He had finally caught on to her waspish mood: She was upset because he'd caught her with her hair down! His eyes narrowed. Why did she hold herself in such tight rein? Why walk such a straight and narrow line?

But a few other questions were entering his conjecture. If Val was really as straitlaced as she had first appeared, why maintain such a glorious head of hair at all? Why didn't she just whack it off and be done with it? And those exercises had been accomplished with supreme grace and fluidity. She was as supple as an elm sapling, and he knew firsthand how firm she was. She had to exercise on a daily basis to be so limber, and that fact combined with her magnificent head of hair didn't quite fit the prudish persona she attempted to convey.

His suspicions were far from distinct, but without a doubt Val LeClair wasn't precisely what she'd been leading him to believe.

Val felt like squirming under his scrutiny and couldn't abide the tension. "I'm going to lock up the models."

"I'll help."

Her lips pursed, but she could hardly tell the owner of the project to butt out.

They walked clear to the end of model row, which was fenced with black wrought-iron so viewers could not run in and out of the area on a whim. At night a security guard patrolled the entire project and watched the models in particular, as the furniture, appliances and decorator pieces in the five houses were worth a great deal of money.

Inside the fifth house, Val began checking windows and doors, carrying on a mental debate as she went. There was really nothing wrong with Rush Saxon learning about her other career—certainly she wasn't ashamed of attaining a certain localized fame. Obviously her desire for a complete break with that aspect of her life had made her a little bit fanatic on the subject.

But her new identity had worked beautifully until Rush came along, and how she lived was no one else's business. Maybe she should have announced her other career to Rush at once. It would be easier to be herself with him now. As it was, she felt some sort of explanation for doing exercises in the sales office and unpinning her hair should be offered, and the thought of explaining herself at this late date was unnerving.

Rush came from the bedroom area. "Everything's secure in there."

"These rooms are secure, also."

They walked to the fourth house to repeat their inspection. "You know," Rush said as they walked in, "this is my favorite floor plan."

Val nodded, relieved to have something besides her embarrassed self to think about. "It's popular with the buyers. There's only one of this model left to sell."

"Where is it?"

"On the corner of Lake and Coker Streets. Near the plaza and fountain."

"Oh, yes." The hundred and ten houses were built around a parklike plaza, which already had a partially completed fountain, and would one day—according to plan—have desert landscaping with walking paths, a little grass for eye appeal, trees and benches.

They went around checking window locks. Val felt a little better, though she wished, heartily, that her hair wasn't flopping around. Every time Rush looked at her, his eyes were on her hair instead of her face, which was damned disconcerting.

He finally went one way and she went the other. Val checked the family room, the living room and the kitchen. Remembering the eccentric lock on the master bedroom's slider, she hastened to that section of the house.

Rush was already there and frowning at the door. "This lock isn't catching."

"It has a mind of its own," Val said dryly. "Let me try. I'm used to it."

Rush stepped aside and Val pushed and pulled the slider until the lock caught. She turned from the door to see Rush staring at her hair again. Only this time, the smoldering light in his blue eyes created a flush in her system that began at her toes and turned her face pink two heartbeats later.

She knew what was coming, and tried to avoid it by ducking around him. He caught her arm. She looked at him. "Don't."

"Why not?" he said softly.

"Just . . . don't," she whispered.

"Val, you're beautiful with your hair like this."

"I didn't unpin it to give you ideas."

"I want to touch it."

"No!" She tried to back up, but he didn't let her. "Please let go of my arm."

"I like you, Val." He tried to draw her closer.

"You *like* my hair," she said inanely, then rolled her eyes. "Let go of me, Rush." But she lamented the huskiness in her voice, because what had been intended as a demand came out sounding like an invitation.

If only he wasn't so handsome, so damned male, she thought wildly, finding herself staring into his shimmering blue eyes. He tugged on her arm, just a little, and she took a tiny step toward him.

His free hand rose to her other arm, and he pulled her forward, very slowly. Then both of his hands rose to her hair, and she saw the muscles in his jaw clench as he wove his fingers into it.

"Fantastic," he mumbled thickly. "Don't ever pin it back again, please."

She swallowed. His scent was overwhelming, coming in waves that threatened her equilibrium. Men do not overwhelm you, she told herself. Move! Get away from him!

But her shoes felt glued to the floor, and the sensation of his hands in her hair was making her dizzy. She gasped in a huge breath of air and realized how revealing it had been by the narrowing of his pupils.

Now he knows, she thought weakly. Now he knows my knees feel like jelly . . . because of him.

He urged her head forward, and she tried to turn her face at the last second. But his mouth touched hers, briefly at first, then again, a solid contact.

She moaned deep in her throat, a combination of protest and pleasure. His lips moved on hers, tasting, teasing, and for a few seconds she couldn't breathe at all.

He raised his head. His eyes were dark and glittering. "Exquisite," he whispered, and dipped his head for another kiss.

Something seemed to explode within her. Her arms came up to lock around his waist. He was warm and real, solid, and so desirable, and she leaned into him, losing herself in the pleasure of his mouth, his tongue.

His hands left her hair to glide down her back, to seek her femaleness through the folds of her sexless gray dress. She felt so differently than she looked in it. Her hips were tight and barely curved, long, lean hips, and long, lean thighs. Her curves were all in her breasts, and the pressure of their fullness against his chest was taking off the top of Rush's head.

His mouth became less gentle, hers became the same. His hand burrowed between their tightly knit torsos to caress one lush breast, and the sensation of it against his palm made him see stars.

He was breathing hard, knocked for a loop by so much unexpected passion, hers, his own. "Val," he mumbled raggedly. "Baby."

She opened her eyes, and in that instant reality hit her. Hard. She backed away from him and pushed at the same time, causing them both to lose their balance. They reeled and steadied themselves.

Her lungs were heaving. "How dare you!"

Her furious, flashing eyes made Rush blink. "Wait a minute. I didn't do that all alone."

Val whirled and headed for the bedroom door. "Finish locking the models by yourself! I'm going home."

Confused, Rush stood there and rubbed his mouth. She was royally ticked, and for what? She'd kissed him back as hungrily as he'd kissed her. The chemistry between them was unbelievably potent. Beneath Val's cool, no-nonsense exterior beat the heart of a passionate woman. Incredible.

Frowning every step of the way, he checked the rest of the models and walked into the sales office. Halfheartedly he emptied disposable cups and dumped them in the trash can. After straightening the brochure rack, he decided the place was good enough.

That's when he spied Val's reading glasses on her desk. She had run off so hastily, she must have missed seeing them. Rush picked up the glasses and wondered if he should just stick them in a drawer. Val would be here again in the morning and might not need them until then.

On the other hand, weren't these glasses the perfect excuse to knock on her door? It was astounding that she'd told him about Larry's condo and neglected to mention she lived only a few doors away. She hadn't mentioned it, he knew, even though he'd been polite when the subject arose.

With a determined look on his face, Rush folded the glasses and tucked them into his shirt pocket. Removing his suit jacket and tie, he walked out of the office with the jacket slung over his shoulder.

Instead of barging right over to Val's condo, Rush used the telephone number she'd written on her business card. He got her answering machine, which puzzled him, as she'd said she was going home.

To kill a little time, he took a shower and got into clean clothes. Larry's condo was great, containing a large-screen TV and a sophisticated CD player. Rush put on some music and tried Val's number again. Still the answering machine. He hung up again without leaving a message.

Though hungry, he was hesitant about eating. If Val agreed, which he was going to do his best to accomplish, they would be eating together. In a restaurant, if she preferred, or here, which he preferred. He'd bought some nice steaks at the market, and salad fixings. Also fruit, whole-grain breakfast cereal and smoked turkey for sandwiches, as he intended eating at home as often as possible.

Barely aware of the music, Rush paced and then tried to call Val again. It occurred to him that she was his only friend in Las Vegas, and that he truly wanted her friendship.

But he couldn't lie to himself about wanting more than friendship from Val. She was so different from any other woman he'd ever taken a liking for, his desire for her amazed him. But he couldn't deny it. His body ached for Val LeClair, and thinking about anything but their heavy-duty kisses in the model just wasn't possible.

By seven he was ravenously hungry and impatient. At eight he gave up, broiled a steak and made a salad, which he devoured in five minutes flat. He called again at nine, ten and at eleven. He finally left a message, speaking coldly, "All of those hang-ups have been me. You said you were going home and I believed you. Apparently something or someone interesting came along and changed your mind. At any rate, I have your reading glasses. You left them in the sales office. I'll bring them with me in the morning. Good night."

Val got home at her usual hour, 1:00 a.m., and went directly to the kitchen for her middle-of-the-night snack. When the teakettle was on the stove, she glanced at her answering machine. The light flashed eight times, which startled her, as that many calls in one evening were unheard of.

"It can happen, apparently," she mumbled, going over to the machine. She frowned through seven hang-ups, and finally heard Rush's message, which angered her. "Jerk," she muttered, and tapped the rewind button.

But she was the jerk, not Rush. Their relationship had become ludicrously convoluted, and for no good reason— simply because she preferred privacy in her personal life. Merely because she had met him as a real estate agent and initially shown him that persona, and doing such a major about-face now would be awkward.

Besides, if the sales on the Saxon Springs project reached completion, she wouldn't have any secrets. Catching an elating glimpse of that sort of longed for freedom in her mind's eye, Val groaned. Would that day ever really come?

Maintaining the status quo was all she could do in the meantime. She'd certainly never anticipated meeting a Rush Saxon when she put on her glasses and took off her makeup to sell real estate. And that aspect of this awful charade was successful. Clients accepted her at face value. No one gushed because she was a celebrity, albeit only in Las Vegas. Husbands didn't leer, and wives didn't get that pinched look because a showroom dancer was after their man.

All she wanted was a normal life, Val thought resentfully as she prepared her cup of herbal tea and slice of cinnamon toast. Was that asking too much?

But Rush didn't understand her—how could he?—and that was disturbing. Her charade was beginning to feel like deceit, and deceiving anyone had been the farthest thing from her mind at its inception. She just hadn't wanted to sell real estate as "Valentine," but would Rush grasp that concept even if she tried to explain it?

After sleeping until 7:00 a.m., Val swam laps in the pool closest to her condo, spent an hour in the workout room and got ready for the day. Again she eyed that multicolored gauze dress in her closet, and again she opted for a nondescript outfit.

Ordinarily she loved Sundays. Two nights away from the Strip were uplifting, and she truly did enjoy talking real estate to prospective buyers. But today she wasn't very keen on holding that open house with Rush. What would they say to each other? After yesterday, there was bound to be strain between them.

She walked into the sales office at five to ten. Silently Rush held out her glasses, and she accepted them with a rather curt "Thank you."

"You're welcome. I would have left them here, but I thought you might need them last night."

"I didn't need them, but thanks for the consideration."

Rush remained standing when she sat at her desk. "You're not going to tell me what you did last night, are you?"

Val's eyes widened incredulously. How did he have the nerve to take that attitude with her? "I honestly don't know what to say to that."

"How about the truth?"

"I was...working," she stammered, shaken that he would be so possessive from a few minutes of intimacy.

"Working at eleven at night?" Rush put his hands on her desk and leaned over it. "Why did you pin up your hair again?"

Val threw up her hands. "Just a damned minute here! I don't take my orders from you, Rush Saxon. I'll work when I want to and fix my hair any way I want to, and if you don't like it, tough!"

"You're working for me!"

"I'm a free agent! Yes, I have an agreement with your company, but that agreement is confined to a specific area, this project! Anything beyond it, and certainly my personal preferences, are none of your business!"

Rush was shaken. He was way out of line and knew it, but Val, with her ludicrous hairstyle and pitiful lack of style, had gotten way under his skin. More so than any woman he'd ever known. What in hell was going on with him?

With his mouth tight and tense, he straightened his back and walked away. Furtively Val watched him go to a window and stare out. His back and shoulders were rigid. From behind he seemed to be fighting some internal battle.

Her own interior was quaking. Their disagreement was senseless. He'd crossed the line with her, and he had no right. She, on the other hand, was a liar and a sneak, and her good intentions had deteriorated into duplicity.

It was an awful mess, bad enough that she nearly blurted out the truth. But she'd been independent for a good many years and didn't like being pushed into a corner by a domineering man.

Rush turned around to face her. "Apparently you're involved with someone." Val's eyes dropped as her uncertainty expanded. "Aren't you going to answer me?"

Her mind raced. Maybe that was as good an excuse as any for her remoteness. Her gaze lifted. "Apparently."

Rush sucked in an unsteady breath. "I got the wrong idea yesterday."

"Yes, you did."

His eyes bored into her. "You kissed me back."

"A mistake," she said evenly. "But not one I want to pay for by destroying our working relationship. I'm sorry, Rush. I apologize for... for yesterday."

It took a minute, but he finally got it out. "I apologize, too. It won't happen again."

With immense relief, Val spotted a car pulling up out front. "Some people are coming in." She got up and went to the brochure rack to be ready for their entrance.

"The models aren't unlocked," Rush said tonelessly. "I'll take care of it."

"Thank you."

He brushed past her and walked out through the side door. Val took a shaky breath and pasted a smile on her face, and when the customers walked in, she said brightly, "Good morning. Welcome to Saxon Springs."

No one could have guessed that her heart felt shattered into a zillion pieces.

Five

On Monday morning Rush passed the word around the construction site that he wanted to talk to everyone on the job, with the meeting to take place in the sales office.

The men filed in silently, though Rush sensed some belligerence in their stoic expressions. He began with "Thanks for coming. I'm Rush Saxon. I think you all deserve an explanation about what's going on with this project.

"First, let me say that I plan to do everything in my power to finish it. I won't insult your intelligence by telling you I've got a fat bankroll and everything's great, because I don't and it isn't. But I do have ideas, determination and what seems like a reasonable plan."

He explained about closing the sales on the models. "...as fast as the title companies can turn out the paperwork. I know you're working shorthanded and that has to change. If you know anyone who left this job to work elsewhere, I would appreciate your contacting them and telling them that

Saxon Springs is back in business. Plus, the money that comes in from any closings will go to labor first.

"I won't pretend to know the construction business. I need advice, and I'll probably be hounding each and every one of you to get it. Try to bear with me. If this project is successful, there will be others. I'm here to stay, and so is Saxon Construction Company."

The men shuffled around and looked at each other. One guy made his way to the front of the group. He spoke up. "We've been trying to keep it together, Mr. Saxon, but I don't mind telling you we're getting damned discouraged. After Dirk walked off, no one knew whether to keep on working or what." He looked at his co-workers for support, then back to Rush. "I guess what I'm saying is, we need our paychecks regular. We all got families, and promises don't put food on the table." A murmur of assent went through the group.

"That they don't," Rush agreed. "But right now promises are about all I have to give you. According to the title companies involved in the closing of the model sales, the company will have money in less than two weeks. I have a little in the bank right now, but not enough to start passing out full paychecks for this many men. But if you could get by on a partial check until those closings, everyone will be paid in full. I guarantee it."

Before anyone could reply too distinctly, Rush added, "There are fourteen houses near completion. Those are the ones to concentrate on. With those fourteen sales, we'll be out of trouble." He smiled with some wryness. "It's a juggling game at this point and I won't try to gloss it over. But I won't take a penny out of the company for myself until every employee has been paid in full."

He scanned the crowd. "It's up to you. Without you, I'll never make it, and every single one of you is thinking exactly that. I'm not begging, because I don't beg. But I am asking you to stay on the job, to accept partial pay until those first closings, and to believe in my sincerity. Thanks for listening."

The men began leaving, and Rush could see them already talking it over. The man who'd acted as spokesman came forward. "I'm Pete Wolinski, Mr. Saxon, one of your carpenters. I want you to know that you've got some good men here."

Rush offered his hand, which Pete shook. "I thought as much, Pete, which is why I'd like to keep them. Do you think they'll stay?"

Pete nodded. "They'll stay. They gotta talk about it for a while, but heck, any company can run into a snag now and then. If you're fair with us, we'll be fair with you. What I wanted to talk about are those fourteen houses you mentioned. There isn't much left to do on 'em except for setting the appliances. A little finish carpentry here and there, but it's the appliances that are holding things up."

Rush didn't know how he was going to obtain fourteen stoves, hoods and dishwashers, but it had to be done. "The appliances will be here, Pete. Count on it."

Afterward, Rush felt a wave of panic. He had just talked very big and had little money and no ideas to back up his bravado.

But the answers weren't in this sales office. Maybe they weren't in the company office, either, but that's where the facts and figures of the project were located.

He locked up and drove the MG the half mile to the company office, hoping Val would be there this morning, as he'd like her input on this problem. She wasn't, but when he sat at his desk, he saw a note from her.

> Rush,
> I got an idea in the night that might help the project, if it works. I should know one way or the other by this afternoon. See you then.
>
> Val

Rush sat back to think. Since yesterday morning, when he'd made a fool of himself with Val, he'd tried to disassociate himself from her on a personal level. At intervals during the open house hours, they had talked about the prospective buyers inspecting the models, but there had been a strain in the air both had been aware of. He'd hoped it would be different today, and maybe it was. Apparently she was still devoted to the project, which was encouraging.

He read the note again, though the message was brief and strictly business. Val was a straightforward, down-to-earth person, obviously not impressed with glamour, content to maintain a low-key life-style.

She didn't deserve to be judged for her preferences, which was precisely what he'd been doing. He'd seen her potential for beauty and denigrated her disregard of it, and he had assumed, because she hadn't socked him over that pass, in fact, had kissed him back with obvious pleasure, that he could expect something from her. She had set him straight in no uncertain terms, and let him know he wasn't the only man in her life.

So be it, he had decided yesterday once his badly damaged ego settled down. He needed to maintain their working relationship, needed Val on the project. Her presence gave him confidence, which he knew he had to have to turn this company's downhill slide around. He'd made a fairly decent start, but operating a business was apparently a constant test of one's ability to solve problems. Knowing that Val was with him, even to coming up with ideas in the night to help the project, was a source of comfort, one that he wouldn't risk again with foolish urges that were probably no more than the natural functional behavior of his hormones.

And speaking of solving problems, Rush thought wryly, he had better stop mooning over Val and get busy on those appliances.

The company's system of record keeping was beginning to make sense to Rush. For instance, he knew exactly where to go in the file cabinet for the folders containing information on appliance vendors. There were half a dozen, and he brought them back to his desk to look through.

There were glossy catalogs touting kitchen ranges and their accoutrements, both electric and gas powered, and brochures for dishwashers. Rush noted prices and did some calculations. Stunned, he laid down his pen: The appliances needed for those fourteen houses would cost more than ten thousand dollars.

Rubbing his forehead, he wondered if either of his brothers had an extra ten thousand, maybe money no one expected to find in the coffers of the businesses they had taken on to operate.

But that idea dissolved at once. This was his problem; Chance and Cash had their own.

He could hock everything he owned and not come up with ten thousand, he knew. His mouth thinned as one last hope took shape in his mind: Buying on credit.

Deciding that he had nothing to lose by asking, he picked up the phone and dialed the local number listed within the glossy pages of an appliance catalog.

Val drove up in midafternoon. From inside the office, Rush watched her get out of her car. She was wearing large black sunglasses, white slacks and an oversize yellow blouse belted at the waist.

A sense of connecting to something solid gripped Rush, as though he'd just been plugged into a source of energy. Val satisfied a need in himself that he hadn't been aware of possessing before coming to Vegas. Maybe the need had blossomed during the past few weeks, when the very foundation of the world as he knew it had crumbled and all but vanished. Whatever, he felt stronger when Val was around than he did when she was absent.

Right at the moment he felt pumped up, merely because he had an astounding story to tell her. He was grinning from ear to ear when she walked in.

She took off her dark glasses. "Hi. Did you see my note?"

"I saw it. Val, you'll never guess what happened today."

She smiled and walked to her desk. "Whatever it was, it put you in a good mood."

"I still can't believe it. Have you heard of Palace Appliances?"

"Sure have. Palace is a major outlet. Why?"

"They agreed to deliver the appliances we need to finish those fourteen houses, with only ten percent down and the balance paid when the sales close."

Val's face lit up. "Fantastic! How did you manage that?"

Rush's grin became a little smug. "My boyish charm, what else?"

"Yeah, right," Val said with a laugh. "Get serious, Saxon. How *did* you manage it?"

"I was honest with them, Val. I told them exactly what was going on with this project, that we had eighty-seven units sold, with twenty-three to go, and no appliances. We must have talked for an hour. Their deal is, they get all the business on the Saxon Springs project, and they'll take care of us during this crunch."

"And you're satisfied with their prices and delivery dates?"

"Completely. A truck will deliver the stoves, hoods and dishwashers for those fourteen units in the morning."

Val was elated. "This is great. What I have to do now is contact those buyers and get those closings rolling." She couldn't stop grinning, and neither could Rush. Accomplishment was heady, and so was sharing it.

"Well," she said after a moment. "I've got some news, too."

"That idea you had in the night?"

"Exactly. I got to thinking about the disadvantage of being without models for the final twenty-three units, worrying about it, actually. And it occurred to me that we might close these first five sales and keep the models, too."

Rush frowned. "I don't see how."

"It's simple. I talked to each buyer, and they're all for it. We go ahead with the closings. You get your money, but the buyers don't take immediate possession. Instead, Saxon Construction Company rents the houses back from the buyers for one month, with an optional month, if needed. Rush, we can use the models for two months, which should be plenty of time to move those last unsold houses!"

"My God," Rush said in utter amazement. "Val, that's the most brilliant idea I've ever heard of!"

"Thank you, but I can't take credit for originating something that's been done before. I'm just glad I remembered the concept."

Rush wanted to hug her. He felt like hugging someone, at any rate. His interior was soaring. Never had he associated such incredible feelings with anything so dry as business, and his mind was expanding, rushing ahead, visualizing goals and successes he couldn't possibly have imagined only a few weeks ago.

"You know something, lady? We're a damned good team."

Val grinned. "Seems so."

Her exhilaration started winding down as the mood in the office began switching. She was suddenly aware of Rush as a man, and from the way he was looking at her, he wasn't thinking of her as merely the other half of that "damned good team."

She had been standing all this time, and she suddenly sat down. "I'm going to start making calls to those fourteen buyers."

"Good idea," Rush said quietly, a little stiffly. He'd known the precise moment that Val had started reading his mind. "We should be ready for a final inspection on those houses in a matter of days. A week at the most."

Val studied the calendar. "How about setting the closing date for..." She hesitated, remembering how many times she had called those same buyers with promises that hadn't reached fruition. "You're certain about the appliances coming tomorrow?"

"If the man's word is good, I'm certain."

"We'll bank on it. Fine, we'll request a closing date for three weeks from today." Val got up and went to a file cabinet for her sales records.

Rush watched her pull the files and carry them to her desk, thinking that no one he'd ever seen moved like Val. Her simplest gesture was like exquisite dancing, appearing weightless, as though she were carried along by a gentle current of air.

A surging desire made him grit his teeth. She's taken, you idiot, he told himself. Don't say or do something else to embarrass both of you.

But today her severe hairstyle and scrubbed face didn't offend his innate taste for glamour. Val was beautiful without cosmetics and fancy clothes, wholesome, real, the most desirable woman he'd ever known. He shoved his hands into his pants pockets to keep from doing something stupid, and walked to his own desk and sat down.

Val glanced at him, but pretended not to notice the tension in the room. She had fourteen important phone calls to make, and it wasn't sensible to assume she would reach every buyer without some second and possibly third attempts. After that would come calls to the involved title companies; she would be busy for hours at the very least, if she even managed to get it all done yet today.

But the thought of sitting here for hours with Rush glowering at his desk only a few feet away—yes, he was glowering—was just too unnerving.

She stood up. "I'm going to take these files home and make my calls from there."

"You are? Any particular reason?"

"Uh . . . then I can take care of some laundry at the same time."

"Fine," Rush said flatly, knowing damned well why Val had decided to avoid him: He made her uncomfortable.

Well, she made him uncomfortable, too, but instead of avoiding her because of it, he wanted to get closer, to learn her secrets, to get to know everything about her. Find out what really went on in her mind, what she did when she wasn't working here, who she was seeing at night. The questions were endless, becoming more complex every day. Val was so blasted closemouthed and private about herself, and he wanted to break through her guard in the worst way.

He knew she wasn't going to allow it, and he'd never faced that sort of frustration before. He sat there and watched her organize her bulky load of files, without offering to help. His soaring mood of a few minutes ago had gone flat, and even knowing that he was acting like a sulky schoolboy didn't alleviate his resentment.

"See you in the morning," Val said as she slung her bag over her shoulder and lifted the files.

"I'll be at the construction site in the morning."

"For the delivery of the appliances."

"Yes."

"Then I'll see you tomorrow afternoon."

She was almost to the door when Rush got control of his ruffled emotions and jumped up. "Let me carry those out for you."

"I can do it. I'll have to carry them in at home, Rush."

He took the files from her arms, and paused to look into her eyes. "I'm sorry."

Val sighed, but she didn't have to ask why he was apologizing. "It's all right. I understand."

His lips set into a grim line. "If you do, it's a hell of a lot more than I can say." His eyes narrowed on her face. "There's something about you I can't quite comprehend, Val. I've heard of mystery women, but I've never met one before."

"I'm no mystery," she scoffed.

"Like hell you're not."

Looking at him at that moment, Val saw only his perfect features and expensive clothes. Yes, he had taken the Saxon company by the horns, but for how long? When he had money in his pocket again, what then?

She'd had her fill of lusting, careless men a long time ago. Rush Saxon was a swinger, if she'd ever seen one. Sure she was attracted to him, what woman wouldn't be attracted to outrageous good looks and oceans of sex appeal?

But she'd be willing to bet almost anything that he would write stupid, arrogant notes to a female performer in a heartbeat, should he take the notion. Without considering what kind of woman she was beneath her feathered and sequined costume, too. Merely assuming she was available because she was an entertainer. He was used to women fawning over him, and the fact that Val LeClair didn't made her a challenge.

She didn't want a man to desire her because she challenged his machismo. That happened every night she was onstage, dammit. She wanted intellectual rapport, a communion of spirit, mutual respect and recognition of those human qualities that went far beyond good looks and sex appeal.

"Give me the files," she said flatly.

"You won't even discuss it," Rush accused.

"There's nothing to discuss! My mysteries are my affair, and, in fact, exist only in your imagination. I'm not saying I don't have a life away from this office because I do, but there's nothing mysterious about it beyond wanting some privacy. You said we're a good team, and I agreed. But good teamwork in business stops right there, Rush."

"Apparently so," he muttered.

"There's no reason for us to argue about anything," she pointed out. "I like working with you, and should you go on to other developments after Saxon Springs, I'd like to be your sales representative."

"But you don't have a lot of faith in my endurance, do you?"

"If you want the truth, no."

"What do you think I'm going to do, take the money when this project's completed and run?"

Val lifted her chin. "I haven't thought that far ahead."

"I don't believe you."

"Believe what you want. Please give me the files."

"I'm carrying them out to your car!"

"Then do it! Stop yammering at me because I don't fit your idea of the perfect woman!"

Rush's jaw clenched. "That's a point we agree on. You're so far from—" Something stopped him: He was going too far again. Mumbling a string of curses, he pushed the door open and stalked to Val's car.

Following, she slapped the dark glasses onto her face and slid behind the wheel. "This bickering is ridiculous! Do you want me out of here? Believe me, you wouldn't have an ounce of trouble in finding another agent."

Rush realized he was trembling. From anger, from frustration. He vowed one thing and did another with Val, over and over again. He was tempted to tell her yes, that he never wanted to see her annoyingly bland face again, but it was so far from the truth, he felt sick to his stomach.

"I'd just as soon complete this project with the personnel on hand," he said coldly.

"Fine. Let's leave it at that," Val snapped as she slammed her door closed.

The scorching sun was burning the top of Rush's head, but he stood there and glared as she drove away. Never had a woman angered him more. Never had he felt such an overwhelming urge to best a woman, to make her say uncle, and in a purring, satisfied voice, to boot.

Someday he would, he vowed. One fine day Val LeClair was going to let down her hair with him, literally. And do a hell of a lot more than that, too. For a second Rush thought of the faceless man in her life with a smidgen of regret, but in the next instant he shoved remorse aside and renewed his vow to best Val just once.

Val was so upset by the time she got home, she nearly drove her car into the back wall of the garage. Stopping just short of a crash, she turned off the key and put her head down on the steering wheel.

The fight with Rush was ludicrous. Not ten minutes before they had been on the same wavelength, elated over their progress with the project. She should despise him. How dare he be so heavy-handed?

His ego couldn't handle rejection, but he was not going to win this battle. She had a right to privacy, and she didn't have to explain her "mystery," either, which was a witless word and infuriating. He only wanted her because she'd brushed him off, the damned egomaniac.

But it wasn't quite that simple, and Val knew it. There was some sort of crazy, wildfire spark between them; she felt it every bit as strongly as Rush did. It was just that he was accustomed to indulging his "sparks," and she was not.

It was a maddening situation. Telling him to find another agent had been nothing more than angry bluster; if he would have taken her up on it, she would have been devastated. Saxon Springs was her baby. She'd worked her tail off and sweated buckets for that project, and seeing it pass to another agent at this point would be a crushing blow.

Juggling the load of file folders, Val finally got out and went into her condo. Its cool interior felt wonderful on her feverish skin, and she soothed her ruffled feathers further with a tall glass of iced tea.

Eventually she started on those calls, but behind every conversation was Rush Saxon's image: He had gotten a lot deeper into her system than she wanted to admit, and if she didn't watch her step very carefully, he was apt to burrow even deeper.

Apparently common sense wasn't a very effective buffer against "crazy, wildfire sparks."

Six

It was getting dark when Val closed the last of the fourteen folders and got up from the telephone desk in her dinette. She snapped on a few lights as she went, and ended up in her bedroom, where she changed into a bathing suit.

With her feet in thongs and carrying a towel, she left her condo and walked toward the nearest swimming pool. She was nearly there when she ran into an elderly couple who also lived in the complex, Vera and Lloyd Chatham.

"Good evening, Val," Vera said with a sweet smile. "Taking a stroll to settle your dinner?"

"I haven't had dinner yet, Vera. I'm going for a swim." Val had a hard time holding a straight face. She was wearing a swimsuit, after all, and it wasn't dark enough yet that Vera Chatham should have missed seeing it.

"Have a nice stroll," Lloyd cheerily called as they separated.

"Thank you." Val chuckled under her breath as she continued down the walk. The Chathams were dear people, but maybe a trifle nearsighted.

There was one person in the pool, Val noticed as she unhooked the gate in the wrought iron fencing and entered the enclosure. The pool lights hadn't yet come on, and the scene was dusky and shadowed. She laid her towel on a chair and kicked off her thongs.

Then she recognized who else was taking an evening swim: Rush. The muscles of her stomach clenched.

But she walked to the edge of the pool and spoke calmly. "I didn't know you were a swimmer."

"I didn't know you were, either," Rush said. Val in a simple white bathing suit was a sight to behold. Her legs seemed endless, the most incredibly long and arousingly shaped legs he'd ever seen on a woman. There wasn't one single bulge in her suit except for her bosom, not the tiniest flaw in the perfection of her sleek, smooth figure.

She dived, a clean cutting of the water's surface that barely created a ripple. The pool lights suddenly flashed on, and in the shimmering aquamarine water, she looked sensuous, like a woman out of a dream. Rush felt slightly shellshocked. Suspecting a perfect body was a long way from seeing it with his own eyes.

Val surfaced. Her smile wasn't very strong, he noted and she realized, but she did her best. "I usually swim laps."

"Don't let me stop you."

Starting at the shallow end, Val set out. Rush leaned against the side of the pool and watched her graceful, steady, overhand strokes. She could outswim him any day of the week, he realized, which grated unreasonably on his nerves.

He wasn't over their altercation earlier today, and he wanted to be. Animosity between him and Val was painful and foolish. When she turned at the deep end for the fifth time, he climbed out of the pool and went for his towel.

Rubbing water out of his hair, he sat on a chair and counted her laps. Ten, and she wasn't even winded.

Eleven...twelve. At the shallow end, Val lowered her feet to the bottom and stood up. She looked around, hoping Rush had gone.

"You're in incredibly good shape," she heard.

Her heart sank—he was still here—but she turned and smiled. "I try." Val walked to the steps, and then wished there were a way to leave the pool without being on full display. It was a strange thought for a woman who wore skimpy costumes in front of hordes of people nearly every night, she knew, but that was professionalism and this was... Well, this was different.

Rush sat perfectly still while she came out of the water, a goddess rising from the sea. He gave his head a sharp, clearing shake and commented a trifle unsteadily, "It's a great evening."

Val reached the chair where she'd left her towel. "Yes, it is." Quickly she took the towel and wiped her face, allowing most of the fabric to hang down in front of her. "I enjoy swimming at night."

"I thought you might be out somewhere."

"Out?"

"With your boyfriend."

"Oh," Val said faintly, recalling his assumption and that she had let him believe it. "I was busy with those calls until a few minutes ago."

"How'd they go?"

"Well enough. The buyers are anxious to close." What she'd run into was a good deal of sarcastic disbelief that those houses would *ever* be ready for occupancy. It had taken some earnest explaining and determined assurances, but the sales seemed secure.

Rush cleared his throat. "About today...I keep getting out of line with you, and I'm sorry."

Relieved to end the strain between them, Val nodded. "I'm sorry, too. Let's forget it ever happened."

"How about letting me make it up to you? I heard you tell those people you hadn't eaten yet, and I'm planning on putting together a shrimp salad for dinner."

Apologies were one thing; going home with him quite another. "Well . . . I'm not really very hungry," she said reluctantly.

"Neither am I. That's why the menu is a salad. I really would like you to join me...unless you have something else to do."

He was insisting, she thought uneasily, and how could she turn him down flat? Today's fight had been silly, and they had to work together. Maybe it was best to go along with his invitation, eat his salad, make some kind of amends and get their business relationship back on course.

"All right, thanks. I'll run home and change. Won't take but a minute."

Rush got to his feet. "I'll go ahead and get things started."

"Can I bring anything?" Val asked as he started out of the pool area.

The gate latched behind him. "Just yourself. See you in a few minutes."

Frowning, she dried off as Rush headed into the dark. There were lights on decorative poles throughout the complex, but standing within the bright pool lights as Val was, everything beyond looked much darker.

He hadn't been exactly friendly, she thought, watching his tall form disappear around the wide curve in the sidewalk. There'd been aloofness and more—maybe resentment—in his voice, if not in his words. Why had he insisted she eat his shrimp salad if he truly felt contentious toward her?

He didn't understand her, but maybe she didn't understand him, either, she thought, unnerved, as she deserted the pool area and headed for home. Why did he keep pressing her? He could have said hello without inviting her to eat with him, even if he had overheard her brief conversation with the Chathams.

Inside her condo, Val got out of her wet bathing suit and stepped into the shower stall. Her hair was already drenched, so she unpinned and shampooed it. But then, as it always did the second she used the dryer on it, it began frizzing. Natural curl was probably a blessing, but hers went one step too far, forming tight coils that were devils to brush out.

But brush it out she did, and also wound it and pinned it securely in place. She dressed quickly then, in faded jeans and a plain white T-shirt, cursing last-minute dates and people who imposed them on other people.

Hiking down to Larry's condo took only a minute, and Rush opened the door almost the second she knocked.

"Sorry I took so long," she said in lieu of a greeting.

"It gave me time to make the salad. Come in."

The table was set, and set very well with Larry's best china and crystal. Determined to make the best of an uncomfortable situation, Val smiled brightly. "Anything I can do to help?"

"Everything's ready. Sit down. I'll bring it in."

Val sank to a chair at the table. "What's that music?"

"Mozart," Rush called from the kitchen. "Do you like it?"

"It's beautiful."

Rush came in with a huge bowl and a bottle of wine. He placed the bowl in the center of the table and the wine next to his place. "I'll get the bread. Be right back."

He returned with a loaf of French bread on a cutting board, which he nestled next to the salad bowl. "There, all set." He sat down and reached for the wine bottle. "Wine?"

"Uh . . . sure. A little. Thanks."

He smiled at her while he poured the chilled white wine into their glasses. "Help yourself to the salad and bread."

"It looks delicious." Val scooped salad onto her plate and then cut off a slice from the French loaf. "Bread?" she inquired, holding out the slice.

"Thanks."

"Hmm," Val said after a bite of salad. "It is delicious. What do you have in here? Do I see sunflower seeds?"

"Sunflower seeds and slivered almonds."

"Wonderful texture," Val said. "And this dressing is different. Did you mix it yourself?"

Rush recited the simple recipe. It was table talk of the dullest order, but he never tried to turn the topic to anything else. They discussed lettuce, of all things, and where to buy the freshest seafood in the city. He'd picked up the shrimp at the supermarket, but didn't admit it.

"Have some more salad."

"I think I will. It's really very good, Rush."

He watched her over his glass. The Mozart concerto swelled to a crescendo on the CD player. The subtle lighting in the dining room reflected in Val's hair, and Rush's fingers ached to free it from those godawful pins.

He judged her as more relaxed than when she'd arrived. It seemed nothing short of miraculous that she was here, sitting across the table, eating with him. Her personality didn't invite familiarity, but right now the "mystery" he'd accused her of fostering wasn't quite so pronounced. It was even possible to think she was enjoying this simple meal with him.

"Pick out the shrimp," he urged as she took another helping of salad and he poured more wine into their glasses.

Val laughed. "Hardly a polite thing for a guest to do."

"I'm not worried about 'polite.' Are you?" His smile was slightly teasing.

She laughed again. "Probably not."

Rush picked up the salad tongs, plucked several plump shrimp from the salad bowl and placed them on her plate. She looked up and smiled. "Thank you."

"Where'd you learn to swim like that?" he questioned.

"We had a pool while I was growing up, so I got plenty of practice."

" 'We' as in your family?"

Val took a swallow of wine, which had a crisp, slightly fruity flavor, tasty with the salad and bread. "My parents. Dad died when I was twelve and Mother died fourteen months ago. She was ill for a very long time."

"I'm sorry. That must have been hard on you."

Val picked up her salad fork. "Do you have any family?"

"Two brothers. I'm the youngest. Our parents were killed in a plane crash when we were very young. Our grandfather raised us."

"You were lucky to have a grandfather who cared. Where do your brothers live?"

"Chance is in Montana and Cash is in Oregon."

"You're all spread out. Too bad."

"Can't be helped. Granddad died only a month ago, and..." Rush cocked an eyebrow. "Do you want to hear this?"

"Yes, of course." Val realized it was true. She'd been curious about Rush's background right from the first.

"Well, it's kind of an odd story. Granddad had a great deal of money, which he made himself. My brothers and I were raised with everything money could buy. Granddad never said no to any request, and in fact seemed to encourage us to live life to its fullest.

"After his death we had the rug pulled out from under us. The money was gone, or so Granddad's attorney informed us. There was very little left of his fortune, primarily three businesses, one in Montana, one in Oregon, and one in Nevada."

Val nodded. "I see what brought you here. You took the one in Nevada. What did the three of you do, draw straws?"

"No, we sat down and talked about it. Actually we made our decision very quickly. We always got along." Rush grinned. "Or maybe I should say, we got along once we grew up."

"You must miss them," Val said, and laid her fork on her plate. "I can't eat another bite. That was the best shrimp salad I ever tasted." She reached for her glass of wine and realized it was empty.

Rush, seeing she'd finished her wine, asked, "Would you like another glass?"

"No, please. Not for me."

"How about some coffee, then." He got up and went to the kitchen where he already had a pot brewing. Efficiently he filled two cups and brought them into the dining room.

Val had a dreamy look on her face when he returned. "That music is wonderful."

"We could sit in the living room and enjoy it," Rush suggested casually, almost afraid to hope the evening would last longer.

Val pushed back her chair. "I really should be going. Let me help with the dishes first."

"You don't have to help with the dishes. What are there, two plates and a salad bowl? It'll take me five minutes to clean up later. Come on. Bring your coffee and we'll sit in the living room."

"Well...all right." In Larry's elegant living room, Val sat on the sofa and Rush chose a chair. She sipped her coffee and asked, "Do you like Larry's place?"

"Sure do. Did he have it decorated by a professional?"

"I really don't know. But it looks like it, doesn't it?"

"Does to me. Is it the same floor plan as yours?" Rush asked.

"Almost. Mine's reversed, and I think Larry's living room is larger. Maybe his unit is a little bigger all the way around," Val mused while scanning the room.

"Have you seen the whole place?"

"Pretty much. Larry usually has the neighbors in for drinks during the Christmas holidays. Of course, I've never seen his bedrooms."

"Do you want to? The guest room is fantastic. Everything is either black or white."

"Really? Sounds rather stark."

"It's not, Val. It's stunning." Rush stood up. "Come and take a look."

Feeling rather conspiratorial, Val lurched to her feet. "Okay, let's see this stunning room of Larry's."

Rush laughed and took her by the hand. He liked her loose, relaxed mood. She always seemed to be on guard, and tonight her guard was down, which pleased him. Smiling, he led her from the room.

Without the slightest protest, she let Rush lead her down a hall to a door, which he pushed open and announced, "*Voilà!* The guest room."

"It's dark. Turn on a light," she demanded in a raspy voice.

"Presto!" Rush pushed the wall switch, and two stylish bedside lamps lit up.

"You're right," Val exclaimed. "It isn't stark at all." The room was gorgeous, mostly white with black accents, furniture, fabrics and walls. The carpet was as white as snow. "I've always loved white carpet," she remarked.

"This is plush stuff," Rush told her. "Take off your shoes and try it barefoot."

His idea seemed inordinately funny, and Val giggled as she kicked off her shoes and took a few steps on the ultrasoft carpet. "It tickles."

Watching her with genuine relish, Rush leaned against the frame of the door. "Something's tickling you. Do you know you have a very nice laugh?"

"Do I?" She laughed again, as if to hear it for herself. Her gaze fell on the dresser, which contained an array of men's toiletries. Her eyes flashed to him. "Is this the room you're using?"

Rush nodded, slowly.

Her laugh this time had a slightly nervous edge. "I shouldn't be in here, Rush."

"Why not?" he asked softly.

"I think you know why not." Val studied the door and the way he was blocking it with his casual slouch against the woodwork. She shoved her feet into her sandals. "May I leave?"

"Do you think I would try to stop you?"

"I...don't know." Val's fingers rose to her temples. "You make my head spin. I'm suddenly feeling very tired."

Rush saw her reeling and leapt forward to steady her. "Easy, honey. Here, sit on the bed for a minute."

"My head hurts."

"Let me fix it, okay?" Sitting beside her, he gently began removing the pins from her tightly bound hair. "Is this helping?"

"Yes," she whispered. Each pin removed relieved the tension in her scalp, and she moved her head languorously, side to side. "That feels good," she said huskily as he worked his fingers through her hair.

"It feels good to me, too," he mumbled thickly.

"What did you say?"

"Nothing important, honey. Just relax and let me do the work." Very gently he massaged her scalp.

She drew in a long, slow breath. "Your hands are pure magic."

"You're magic, Val," he whispered, lifting her hair to press his lips to the back of her neck.

A tingling shiver went through her, intensified by the kisses he feathered along her hairline. She tried to hang onto reason and whispered, "I shouldn't be here...not like this." Not sitting on his bed with him. Not with him toying with her hair and kissing her neck.

But it all seemed hazy, rose-tinted and lovely, happening to her most sensuous self, to the side of her she kept private and away from the public eye.

Rush was completely lost in her scent and the exquisite curve of her nape. He let her glorious hair fall over his face and basked in its smell and texture. Slowly his mouth moved from the back of her neck to her ear, where he nipped at her lobe. He kept feeling her response, recognizing it in her languid movements and short breaths.

But he'd also heard her vague objection and experienced a flutter of conscience. His vow to best her seemed senseless now. That had nothing to do with this, he thought with some vehemence, as though someone had accused him of entrapment. Wanting Val so desperately now was in no way connected to his anger earlier today. This was beautiful, meaningful, and he hadn't planned it.

"You're so special, Val," he whispered. "I've never known anyone like you." Within the tangles of her hair, his lips moved up her cheek to her temple.

She was trying to think, to get her senses beyond the thrills compounding in her body. "But . . . you have to stop kissing me."

"Why, baby? Kissing is good. So good." His lips slowly crossed her forehead.

His voice was mesmerizing, and his warm breath on her face was intoxicating. Her hand rose to his arm for support, as it was becoming difficult to remain upright when her body felt so weak and limp.

He was in tune with her every heartbeat. "Here, honey, lie back." Tenderly he brought her down to the bed, and because her lips were parted and so irresistibly inviting, he kissed her.

Val sighed at the sensation of his mouth on hers. It was a gentle and undemanding kiss, slow-moving, warm, only slightly wet. And so delicious. So very, very pleasurable. She felt his tongue slide lazily over her lips, and it seemed like the most marvelous idea in the world to lie there and enjoy it.

As though from afar, she felt his leg glide up and over hers. He pressed closer and lifted himself to an elbow to look at her. He wore a faint smile, she saw, and the warm affection in his eyes brought a small smile to her own lips. She watched his head slowly descending, his handsome face coming closer, and she shut her eyes for another sweet, gentle kiss from him.

Her left hand languidly rose to the back of his head, where she caressed the crisp strands of his hair. His tongue slipped into her mouth, and her tongue willingly met it. The kiss became heavier. She felt him pressing her deeper into the bed. Her mind spun faster, but her headache was definitely gone.

His weight was thrilling, and Val couldn't seem to find the strength to push him away. Everything was happening in slow motion, his drugging kisses, her own movements. She could feel the rigid flesh behind his fly against her hip, and knew, somewhere in the dim recesses of her mind, where this was going. And yet she wasn't able to break away from Rush, not when each erratic beat of her own heart urged her to snuggle closer.

Her erotic little slide to get nearer raised Rush's blood pressure. His mouth opened on hers in a hungry kiss. A husky moan came from her throat as her own hunger built. She wriggled against him and threaded her fingers in his hair, unable to tell any longer where one kiss left off and another began.

They curled together, a sensuous maze of legs and arms. Rush whispered how sweet she was, how desirable, and the lovely words wrapped around her brain and ignited her passion. Her hands moved to his chest, while his glided down her body to her thighs and then up to her breasts. He bent to kiss the soft contours of her breasts through her T-shirt and then couldn't resist their exciting crests, where he lingered and teased until she moaned again.

"May I?" he whispered, and lifted the hem of her T-shirt. With the shirt bunched above her breasts, Rush laid his face within the cleavage between the cups of her bra. He inhaled deeply and thought her dewy skin smelled like wildflowers. His heart was pounding so hard he could hear it in his own ears. Val was everything a man could want in a woman—beautiful, sensual and with one trait that made her outstandingly different from the other women he had known: She possessed old-fashioned tendencies.

That newly realized knowledge swooped through him, elating him. Why hadn't he seen her disregard for paint and perfume for what it was? Plain, old-fashioned decency. Yes, it made her seem prim and prudish when compared to the short skirts and made-up faces so many women preferred. But Val's values were the kind a man hoped for in a wife, in a life partner.

This was her only mystery, he realized as his excitement mounted. She didn't come on to every man she met. Her standards were higher than what he was used to, which should be prized rather than denigrated.

And she couldn't be in love with that other guy and be so responsive to him. His desire for her flamed. Having lain down from a sitting position, their feet were dangling over the edge of the bed; they needed to get more comfortable. "We're sideways," he whispered against her lips. "Let's turn around and move up on the bed."

Val's hand went to the elegant white spread. "We shouldn't be lying on Larry's spread."

"Easily remedied." Everything was easy, he realized with a staggering elation as he drew her up from the bed, threw the spread back and directed her to lie down again, this time with her head on a pillow. He felt such enormous tenderness for her that his hands trembled as he slid off her sandals and dropped them on the carpet.

Val was as pliant as putty and starry-eyed with desire. She watched him remove his shirt with a dazed half smile, and when he lay beside her again, she was waiting with opened arms.

Their kisses were no longer gentle. Fevers were rising. Val stroked his chest, his shoulders, his back, and he managed to get her T-shirt over her head and then unhook the clasp of her bra. Her naked breasts nearly undid him, but he vowed her pleasure would come before his own.

Each step of undressing her brought pleasure. He kissed her breasts, her abdomen, and as her jeans and panties were slowly pulled down, he kissed her hip bones. Val, herself, kicked away the last of her clothes. Rush quickly shed his slacks and briefs, and returned to take her nude body into his arms with a ragged groan.

His throat was so full of emotion, he honestly couldn't speak above a whisper. Almost crazed from an overwhelming need of her, he kissed her wildly and became even more frenzied from her passionate, uninhibited response.

They writhed together, kissing and touching each other. Val's hungry hands traveled down his torso to his manhood, as his went to the moist heat between her legs. She whimpered hoarsely as he boldly caressed and tantalized, and then moved her legs farther apart to kiss her intimately.

Neither wanted to rush things, but the pressure was becoming unbearable. "I...can't take any more," Val moaned. "Do it. Make love to me."

Rush reached into the bed stand drawer for protection, which he took care of quickly. Nature dominated then, nature and the burning need in Rush's gut. He slid into his passionate lady while kissing her lips, taking her first gasp of pleasure into his own mouth.

It was wild and hot, a trip to the stars, accompanied by groans and growls and a squeak in the bed that Rush hadn't noticed before. But he wasn't thinking about squeaks or anything beyond the incredible perfection of their union. They fitted together as though by mystical design, and the clearest thought of all in his passion-dazed mind was that they had been destined to be together.

He felt Val's climb to fulfillment, and the exact moment she went over the edge. Freed from the control he had inflicted upon himself, he let himself go and came to a roaring climax. Drained and utterly sated, he collapsed.

Val collapsed, as well. She possessed no energy at all and barely the ability to think. It seemed forever before she was even able to open her eyes, and certainly she preferred keeping them closed. To sleep now would be the height of luxury, she thought. To simply curl up and drift off, which every cell of her body was urging her to do.

She felt no regret, no remorse. Their passion had been beautiful, a memory to cherish. She finally stirred. "Rush?"

He raised his head and gazed at her through blissfully satisfied eyes. "Yes, my love?"

That's when she became a little uneasy. "I . . . need to get up."

His smile was radiant. "Am I getting heavy?"

She latched onto the excuse. "Yes."

Before he let her go, his mouth sought hers for another kiss, this one rife with contentment.

Val slipped away, gathered her clothes and went into the bathroom. Her head was still spinning, but from different causes than before. Their lovemaking had gone far beyond the ordinary, and she couldn't muster any regret for the most exhilarating experience of her life.

But that's where her problem lay, as well. She and Rush were teetering on the very edge of emotional commitment, and he didn't know her! He thought he did, he believed the side of Val LeClair he had seen thus far was all there was, and only she could set him straight.

Val dressed hurriedly, breathlessly, with her heart pounding and her mouth dry. This amazing relationship could go no further until she told Rush about Valentine. But when? The thought of doing it right now made her physically weak. She wasn't ready for confessions and confidences, for trying to explain that she hadn't meant to deceive anyone with her real estate persona.

Tomorrow, she promised herself. Or very soon. But not tonight. Tonight she had to go home and think about what had just taken place.

Seven

Rush couldn't understand Val's haste to leave and said so, which resulted in a rather frozen expression on her face. Unresigned and perplexed, he ignored her polite protests and walked her home, then returned to his condo, puzzled and worried. She wasn't angry, he gratefully reminded himself while putting the kitchen in order. But what *was* she feeling? He'd been on the verge of a serious conversation, something along the lines of "What's happening to us is important, Val. I've never felt like this with anyone else."

Maybe she'd suspected what was on his mind and wasn't ready for that sort of discussion, but he couldn't stop asking himself, why not? Was she more involved with that nameless guy than he'd been thinking? Maybe feeling guilty because of him?

The conjecture ripped Rush apart. He had fallen hard and fast for Val, and just when he thought he'd solved her mystery, she threw him another curve.

He lay in bed and became aroused again from just thinking of her beautiful body. It still didn't make a whole lot of sense to him that she wasn't at least a little prideful of her physical perfection, but there was something deeply satisfying about her extreme modesty, all the same. The man who captured Val LeClair's heart would never have reason to wonder about her loyalties. She was an old-fashioned girl, preferring plain over fancy, calm over storm.

And beneath her unassuming, reserved exterior she was passionate and sexy, a dynamite combination. Considering Val's many assets from every conceivable angle, Rush wanted her more than ever. He would have to court her as a gentleman did a lady, he decided. Tonight had been a fluke, if a very telling one. She was as drawn to him as he was to her, but she never would have let him know if things hadn't progressed as they did.

He would ask her out for tomorrow evening. Something simple, as "simple" was all he could afford. Maybe a movie, or merely a drive somewhere. Val had to know the local sights, and she might enjoy showing them to him.

Planning an old-fashioned courtship, Rush drifted off to sleep.

Val wasn't quite so fortunate. All along she'd suspected Rush was trouble, though she never could have devised this scenario in her wildest dreams. She was falling for him, which was crazy given her dislike of too-handsome men with a bit too much ego. Maybe that was fine; it was probably time she met a man who could turn her inside out in the bedroom.

But why, in God's name, had it happened in this way, with her focused on real estate and determined to put "Valentine" behind her? Rush's every impression of her was of her own making, and explaining herself now would make her look like a liar. Visualizing herself telling him that she wasn't really the staid businesswoman she'd been projecting, but a stage dancer who was *trying* to become successful in a whole other arena, was actually frightening. Rush's opinion of her was set; Val LeClair, real estate agent, was the woman he cared for, *not* Valentine, the featured dancer in the Casbah's main showroom!

Sick at heart, Val put in a restless night and awoke in the morning to contemplate running away from the whole mess. Leaving Las Vegas and both careers, and starting over somewhere else had a coward's appeal, if none other. She wasn't completely in love with Rush yet, but she was close. As disheartening as that prospect was, it wasn't nearly as bad as Rush thinking he was falling in love with her and becoming disillusioned and hurt when he discovered her background. And her dread had nothing to do with shame or embarrassment over dancing onstage, either. It was that her penchant for privacy felt like lies now, and she honestly didn't know how to rectify her mistake in judgment without looking like a liar and a schemer.

Val finally got out of bed vowing to avoid Rush as much as she could; it was her only sensible approach to the problem. Total avoidance was impossible, of course. As long as she was involved with the Saxon Springs project, she would have to see Rush on an almost daily basis.

But there would be no more temptations between them. No more intimate dinners in Larry's condo, and certainly not in hers. When her break was clean and final with the Casbah—not too far away now, with the closings finally underway—then she would explain everything to Rush and hope he understood.

Busy at the construction site all morning, where two large trucks lumbered in to unload their cargo of kitchen appliances, Rush nevertheless kept an eye peeled for Val's car. She never showed, and his concern for her attitude intensified.

He delivered invoices and related information to Lois at the accounting firm, spent time at the company office to go over estimates of completion dates and costs on every house in the project and finally faced Val's absence for what it was: If she wanted to see him, she would be here. When he reversed that theory, it was clear that she *didn't* want to see him, and why in hell not?

Seated at his desk, Rush threw down his pen with a grim curse. Thinking he'd figured Val out last night and being so wrong was a kick in the ego, which she was damned good at administering. He didn't know where he stood with Val, and it was darned odd that she could run so hot and cold with a man.

It also wasn't fair, and he wasn't going to accept it and do nothing. Angrily he reached for the phone and punched out her home number. He got her answering machine, and when it beeped for his message, he said, forcefully, "Val? If you're there, pick up. This is Rush, and I need to talk to you."

She came on the line. "Hi."

He released the breath he'd been holding. "How're you doing?"

"Fine."

"Expected to see you here today. Anything wrong?"

"I've been busy with the project's buyers. On the phone most of the day."

"I thought you reached everyone yesterday."

"There are eighty-seven buyers to keep informed, Rush, not just the fourteen whose houses are nearing completion. And the new sales from the weekend required some calls, as well."

"I see." His voice warmed some. "Then there's nothing wrong with us?"

Val cleared her throat. "Of course not."

Relief flooded Rush's system. "Great," he said quietly. "I should be leaving here in about thirty minutes. Let's have dinner together and then do something. Take a drive, maybe."

"Rush, I can't. Thanks for asking, but I just...can't."

The conversation was making Val ill. Tonight began her five consecutive nights of performances, and Rush was apt to suggest seeing her every one of those evenings. How was she going to deal with this? He cared about her, he wanted her, and Lord help her, she wanted him, too. But she couldn't force an explanation out of her mouth yet, and especially not on the phone.

Rush raked his hair as he struggled with her refusal. He finally emitted a feeble laugh. "You've got me very confused, Val."

"Not intentionally."

"But you're not going to tell me what else besides business and me occupies your time, are you?"

Val's mind raced, considering and discarding trumped-up excuses that might keep her busy in the evening. In the end, she just couldn't fabricate a story about taking classes at the university, or visiting a sick friend.

"Rush, we're working together. It's just not sensible to risk that necessary relationship with something personal. Later on, when the project is finished—"

Stunned, Rush interrupted. "After last night, you're saying you don't want to see me outside of working together? Val, there's something going on you're not telling me. Is it that other guy?"

"What other...? Oh, God, no," she groaned, then wished she had let him go on believing in a completely nonexistent person. "There's no other guy," she said wearily, exhausted from a long day of self-castigation and self-doubts, and tons of remorse for merely being herself. She shouldn't have to explain herself to anyone. She had a right to keep her two careers separate, and why couldn't she just tell Rush what she had tried to do and forget it?

Because *he* wouldn't be able to forget it, she realized again. He believed she was one kind of woman, straitlaced, serious, maybe even a goody-goody, and he was bound to see her charade as deceit.

"There's no other guy," Rush echoed flatly, without believing her. "Then what are you doing tonight?"

An offensive was her only defense, Val thought numbly. He wasn't going to let her off the hook any other way. "My evenings are my own, Rush, and last night gave you no right to pry."

Rush's voice dropped to a dangerously low level. "What did last night give me then, if no rights? Should I think you take your pleasure wherever you find it, and that one man means no more to you than any another?"

Her throat was suddenly full and choking. "Do I really deserve that?"

Some of his tension relented. "Probably not, but do I deserve what you've been dishing out? I thought last night meant something." When she remained silent, he added, bitterly and with growing anger, "Guess not. Tell you what, honey. The next time you feel like indulging in shrimp salad and hot sex, come by the condo. I'm probably too damned dumb to say no."

Val stiffened. "That's enough, Rush! You've succeeded in making me angry, and I'm not going to listen to any more insults. You listen to me for a minute. I intend to see every one of my sales at Saxon Springs through to completion, which means we're going to have to communicate. Let's try to keep it civilized, okay?" She slammed down the phone.

Wounded and furious, Val paced her condo. Hours later, when she left in her car to drive to the Casbah, she was still wounded and furious.

But later on, arriving home in the middle of the dark and silent night, she was only wounded.

At the company office the next morning, they spoke only when necessary and very politely. But there was something that Val had to bring up concerning the project, which required a bit more conversation.

"I'd like to keep the models open every day again," she began. "I did that for months before Dirk left, and it had a positive result. A lot of buyers shop during the week, and we have twenty houses left to sell."

"And you'd like to get this project wrapped up and out of your hair," Rush said coolly.

"Wouldn't you?"

"Yes, but *I* need the money."

"Well, why on earth do you think I'm beating my brains out, if not for money?" she retorted sharply.

"Are you short of money?"

"Since you asked, yes. Nearly every penny I earned for seven years went to pay for my mother's medical care, and there are a lot of bills yet to pay."

The concept of old debts startled Rush. Except for his current roster of construction bills, he'd never owed money to anyone. "I'm sorry," he said with sincere sympathy. "Didn't your mother have any insurance?"

"Her insurance was canceled after an operation."

"Can they do that?"

"Apparently so."

"Did you fight their decision?"

"I filed a complaint with the Nevada State Insurance Commission, but Mother's final and fatal condition was something excluded in the original policy, Alzheimer's disease. I'm sure you've heard of it. Anyway, the commission ruled that the company had to pay any costs related to the operation she had, but as Alzheimer's disease was excluded from the coverage, they could do nothing for me."

"That's really rough," Rush commented.

"Once Mother's own money ran out...well, someone had to pay the bills." Val disliked the topic, and she rarely discussed it with anyone. She had loved her mother, and had suffered at her deterioration. Complaining about her medical bills seemed disloyal to Val, because she would gladly have taken on any amount of debt to make her mother well again.

"Anyway," she said, pointedly changing the subject. "Do I have your permission to keep the models open every day?"

Silently Rush looked at her. Wearing that plain gray dress again and with her hair so severely styled, it wasn't easy to tie Val to the beautiful, uninhibited woman in his bed the other night. Yet he knew what that sexless gray dress concealed so well, and exactly how incredible she looked with her hair free and tangled around her face.

"You have my permission," he said quietly. "Why would I withhold it?"

Val turned away. She didn't know why Rush might do anything, nor why she, herself, did some of the things she did. Like going to his condo to eat with him. Surely she should have suspected there was more on his mind than shrimp salad. He had probably invited her while plotting seduction, the cad.

They worked in silence for nearly an hour, Val at her desk checking sales files, Rush at his, going over cost factors again.

At noon he stood up. "I'm going for some lunch. Would you like something brought back?" He wished she would invite herself along. It wouldn't be much, probably a half hour in a fast-food restaurant, but anything would be better than what he had now.

"No, thanks," Val replied. "I'm not staying much longer."

Rush's face tightened. "Fine. See you later, if you're still here."

Val watched him go to his topless little car through the front window. The sun was searing, and it had to be well over a hundred degrees outside. On impulse she jumped up and ran to the door. "Rush, if you want to take my car, go ahead."

He looked at her with very little emotion. "Why would I do that?"

Val's face flushed. "Because it has air conditioning."

"Thanks, but mine'll do." He settled onto the scorching leather seat without a wince and started the MG's engine, and he drove away with the satisfaction any stubborn fool would get out of refusing a kindness from someone with whom he was angry.

Val was making him crazy, and he didn't like it. He didn't like watching every word and tiptoeing around anyone, but particularly not around a woman who had the ability to pin his thoughts on sex and make him ache in the process.

When the project was finally sold-out, it would be over. He would assist with the daily open house whenever possible, and do anything else he could to shorten the duration of their relationship. And when that day came, he just might have a few choice words to lay on Ms. Val LeClair.

Tired but restless, Rush took an after-dark jog that same night. There were acres of sidewalks and streets within the stuccoed block walls of the huge condo complex, and Rush covered most of them. He was heading back to his own area when he spotted Val's car driving out through the front gate.

Breathing hard from running, he leaned over and placed his hands on his knees, pausing to wonder where she was going. It took a minute to realize he was torturing himself with speculation about that other man again. He had never felt jealousy before in his life, and it was a physically painful sensation. Grimacing, he straightened up and headed for home, fast, thinking that he needed something, or someone, to get his mind off of Val.

Inside his condo, he wiped his sweating face with a towel and contemplated his nearly empty wallet. About the only thing he could afford to do was watch other people spend *their* money. Disgustedly, he tossed the towel.

On Wednesday morning, Val opened the models for the public. She had already strung signs along the road announcing the open house, so she was ready for business when she unlocked the doors.

She sat and waited. The first lookers didn't arrive until just before noon, and the morning had been long and empty, giving her more than enough time to assess her entire life, from childhood through the present.

Rush was important. That fact kept rising above all others and tying her in knots. She hadn't wanted him to be. She had done everything she could to discourage his interest, but all of her objections to any man without deeply embedded roots, who also possessed an overly inflated ego, were fading into obscurity. She had never believed that love closed one's eyes to faults and flaws, but she was beginning to believe it now. Rush Saxon was far from perfect, if one discounted his remarkable looks. He'd proven his temper several times, he was the product of a wealthy, indulgent grandfather—by Rush's own admission—and if he had a future in Nevada, it was hanging by a very slender thread.

She, on the other hand, was one for long-range planning. Upon deciding on a job in real estate, her instinct had been to abolish all ties with her dancing career. It still seemed sensible, but her reasons for feeling that way weren't quite as distinct as they'd been. It took some doing to dredge up the simpering leers on the faces of men in the showroom audience, and to recall the lewd catcalls, and the awful notes. There were positive aspects of performing, of course, but she was long past enjoying them.

But would Rush understand the revulsion she felt at such crudity? There were other women in the business who felt as she did, but a good many of them laughed it off and said it came with the territory and didn't matter. There was a time when Val had laughed it off, as well, and she had to wonder when and why she had lost her former resiliency. Perhaps it had happened when her mother became so ill, and the serious side of life had hit her so hard.

Sighing, Val welcomed the sight of another car arriving. Rehashing her relationship with Rush only came to the same dead end every time: There was nothing but heartache in store for either of them until her day of confession, and Val simply could not bare her soul until the house sales were closed, she had money in the bank and "Valentine" was no more.

What pained her was the possibility that complete honesty with Rush would only assure her of permanent heartache. In the end, it was going to be all up to him.

Rush came into the sales office that afternoon. "Any customers?"

"A few."

"There should be more tomorrow when the newspaper ad comes out."

Val nodded. "I'm sure that will make a difference." Being in the same room with Rush was disturbing. She couldn't look at him without thinking of the night they made love. Her love life was nothing to boast about, probably her own fault. But she had met too many of the wrong kind of men not to be calloused on the subject, and even a little prejudiced. To be perfectly honest, she wasn't all that certain Rush was any different.

But he reached her, whether he was another Mr. Wrong or the elusive Mr. Right. The last thing she wanted was to be a fool for love, to be swayed by good looks and sex appeal, but she feared it was happening regardless.

Right now, for instance, she thought he looked gorgeous in pale blue slacks and a casual white shirt. Val had never seen a better dresser than Rush. His lean body was perfect for the latest styles, and he wore clothes with a confident flair.

But his confidence was questionable at the moment, she realized uneasily. He was shifting his weight and trying to look nonplussed, and if he started grilling her again, it was apt to end up bad, as she was in no mood for another question and answer session.

She began puttering with items on her desk. "Are you going to be here?"

"Be here? As in what?" he asked.

"As in being here until closing time. If you are, I'll run and take care of some errands."

"Valid errands, or something you just came up with to get away from me?"

"Honestly!" she exclaimed angrily, and stood up to gather her things. "Why do you insist on picking fights? Do you enjoy hostility?"

His hands clenched at his sides. "Do you know what I'd like better than anything else from you? A little honesty."

Val swallowed the panic welling in her throat. If he pushed too hard, he might hear more honesty than he wanted, which would absolutely destroy her right now. She needed her ducks in a row before attempting candor, and not one blessed thing was in order yet.

"Be careful what you wish for," she cautioned darkly as she slung her purse over her shoulder. "You just might get it."

"What's that supposed to mean?"

"It means that nobody's perfect, Rush." Val stopped at the door. "Be sure to lock up. I'll be here in the morning."

He wanted to ask her where she went at night so badly, his teeth ached. But all he said was, "Fine. See you tomorrow."

But after she'd driven away, he stood at a window and felt sick to his stomach. His feelings for Val were neither funny nor trivial, and nothing in his life had prepared him for the frustration of loving a woman who didn't love him in return.

Her "old-fashioned" tendencies were a crock, apparently. Old-fashioned women didn't run around at night, not where he came from, at least.

Rush's mouth tightened in self-disgust. *That* cynical observation had been the biggest crock of all. He didn't know any old-fashioned women and never had.

Eight

By Sunday Val was more than ready for two nights away from the Casbah. The daily open house at the project was tiring, but two solid sales made the effort worthwhile. As hoped for, the newspaper ad increased buyer activity, and Sunday was particularly hectic. Val was glad to lock up the models at four, and anticipated a quiet evening at home before a good long night of sleep.

At intervals Rush had been in and out of the sales office all day. A crew of men was working at the construction site, and the progress of the fourteen houses was uppermost in his mind. He made a point of watching the time, however, and when the clock neared four, he returned to the models to help Val lock up.

He found her wrestling with the sticky lock on the slider door in the fourth unit. "I've been meaning to get that repaired," he told her as he strode into the room.

She looked up. "The darn thing is getting worse."

"Let me try it."

"Be my guest." Val backed away from the slider. While Rush fiddled with the lock, she checked the rest of the house and then returned to the bedroom. "Did you get it to work?"

"Take a look at it, Val. Is that screw supposed to be sticking out like that?"

Val brought her head down to peer at the balky lock. "Hmm. I don't know. Will it tighten?"

"I tried to tighten it with my pocketknife, but it won't turn."

"Maybe it's stripped. We can't leave the place unlocked, Rush. Are any of the men still working?"

"They were a few minutes ago. I'd better go find someone to fix this."

"I'll get everything else locked," Val called as Rush sped away.

She had worked her way through the number three and number two units when she spotted a carpenter leaving with a handful of tools. "Did you get the lock fixed?" she asked him.

"All fixed," the man announced.

"Thanks." Val looked around. "What happened to Rush?"

"He was still in the number four unit when I left."

Val followed the man to the outside door of the sales office and let him out, then locked it and wondered what was keeping Rush. With everything secure, there was no reason to linger in the models.

Unless, she thought, he hadn't heard her comment about checking the rest of the units while he fetched the carpenter. Maybe he was doing the same thing. Sighing, Val went to look for him.

He was still in the master bedroom of the fourth unit, standing at the slider with his back to the room. From the doorway she watched him for a moment. He seemed completely lost in thought, and she wondered if his intense concentration had anything to do with her. They had been communicating only when necessary and about nothing personal, but she'd felt his eyes on her often, burning with curiosity, and she didn't like being the cause of any discomfort for him.

"Rush," she said quietly. "What are you doing?"

Rush turned. "I thought you'd gone."

"Everything's locked. We can both leave."

"I'm in no hurry. You go ahead."

Was he feeling sorry for himself? Certainly he sounded lonely. Whom did he know in Vegas besides her and the construction workers? That wasn't her fault; it was up to a newcomer to any area to get out and meet people.

But he was so involved with the project, and he hadn't tried to conceal his lack of funds. Val felt a wave of compassion. Rush Saxon was not her responsibility, but neither was he an ordinary acquaintance.

"Uh...Rush..." Val stopped herself. What was she doing? Suggesting some activity together for this evening would be an open invitation. Rush would probably take it that way, at any rate.

"What?" He was looking at her, quizzically, Val saw.

She fidgeted with the clasp on her purse. "Nothing, really. I guess I was just concerned about you. Are you all right?"

Folding his arms across his chest, Rush leaned against the wall next to the slider. "Why would you be concerned about me?"

His macho defensiveness annoyed Val. "Everyone gets lonely at times, even big tough men," she said with some sarcasm.

"I'm more perplexed than lonely," he stated evenly. "I can't figure you out."

Val rolled her eyes. "Please don't tell me you're wasting your time on that dull occupation."

"And don't *you* tell me there isn't anything *to* figure out," Rush retorted. He lifted his hand to point a forefinger at her. "You're hiding something and calling it your right to privacy. If I didn't care about you, it wouldn't mean a damn, but I do and it does. You can't change that by ignoring me, Val.''

"I've hardly been ignoring you. We see each other every day,'' she pointed out.

"At work. But several times this week I've seen you leaving the complex at night. Where do you go, Val?''

She was stunned. "I can't believe you would actually spy on me!''

"I haven't spied, dammit!'' Rush pushed himself from the wall. "But I can hardly miss seeing your car when it drives right past me.''

Val's stomach was churning. This had gone far enough. However he took it, it was time he learned the truth. She opened her mouth to release the torrent of words burning her brain, but nothing came out. Trembling, she turned away and walked to a bureau, where she laid her hands, palms down, on its cool surface and let her head drop forward.

Rush frowned. "Val?''

"Please go away,'' she mumbled. "Leave me alone.''

"What's wrong?'' Rush moved closer, and then closer still, until he was standing right behind her. Her slumped shoulders caused a ponderous, sorrowful feeling in the pit of his stomach. "What did I do to make you feel so bad?''

"You push too hard, Rush. We've known each other for what, two weeks? Two weeks doesn't give anyone the right to push someone else so hard.''

"Asking a few questions isn't pushing, Val.'' He laid his hands on her shoulders and massaged the tension he felt in them. She flinched at first, then stood there and let him do it.

There were a lot of things she'd like to let him do, she thought wearily as his hands moved over her back and shoulders. How could she fight him and herself, too? All week, since last Monday night, she'd kept things cool between them. More than cool, cold. She'd tried not to see the smoldering, curious looks he'd laid on her at every opportunity, overlooked his anger and outright insults, denied her own feelings again and again, and for what? All he had to do to undermine her every ploy was to touch her.

They were alone in this beautiful bedroom, he knew it, she knew it. The outside doors were locked, and they were the only ones with keys. Rush's first step on the road to seduction—of which Val was well aware—was to take down her hair. She closed her eyes as he began removing pins.

It wasn't too late to stop this, she thought with some panic. If she let him go on, there would be nothing nor no one to blame but herself. Rush didn't want just a few kisses.

Heaven help her, she wanted the same thing, the two of them naked, lying together, making love together. She shivered, not because she was cold but because she was suddenly besieged by a raging fever.

Rush dropped his handful of hairpins on the bureau, and said, low and huskily, "Turn around, Val."

She turned, slowly, to look into his heavy-lidded blue eyes. He slid the strap of her bag from her shoulder, placed the bag on the bureau and said softly, "I'm going to close the drapes."

The drapes swished shut, and the room became shadowy. Rush returned to place his hands on each side of Val's face. "Tell me you want this."

Her lashes fell for a moment, then lifted. "I want it."

His lips brushed hers. "I want you so much I hurt." His fingers wove through her hair. "Maybe this is all that really matters, Val," he whispered as his mouth settled on hers.

She groaned and wrapped her arms around him. Her mouth opened for his tongue, and he pressed his lower body into hers. The bureau was at her back, its edge biting into her hips. Kissing her all the while, Rush lifted her skirt and went into her panties. "Open your legs," he hoarsely whispered against her lips. "Let me touch you."

As with their first time, Val could deny him nothing. What he wanted, she wanted, and at the first touch of his fingers on her most sensitive spot, her senses were bombarded with a blinding release. Whimpering, she clung to him, her face buried in his shirt.

"Baby," he whispered raggedly. Deeply moved by her responsiveness, he held her and caressed her back with long, sweeping strokes of his hand. When she was calmer, he tipped her chin and looked into her eyes. "Are you still with me?"

Her voice was low and trembling. "I'm with you."

Rush was trembling, too. The first sharp edges of Val's desire had been soothed somewhat, but his were reaching astronomical proportions.

He glanced behind to the bed then back to Val. "Does that bed have bedding?"

"A mattress cover," she whispered.

"Good enough." With their arms around each other, they stumbled to the bed. Val saw it coming closer, as though it were doing the moving instead of them. She was dazed and knew it. Very dazed, very strung out. She had to be in love with Rush for him to affect her so strongly, she thought dimly. If he asked her anything right now, she would not be able to elude honesty.

But honesty between them would feel good, and she hoped he would mention her evasiveness again.

He didn't. He wasn't thinking of anything beyond the moment, beyond the urgency in his body. He let go of Val to draw back the heavy decorator bedspread, but he returned to her at once and began working open the buttons on her dress.

She did the same with his shirt. Their hands weren't steady and they tried to hurry, to undress each other while exchanging frantic, breathless kisses.

Their clothing pooled on the floor, forgotten. Naked, they tumbled to the bed. She opened her legs for him at once, needing him now. He took only a second for protection and then positioned himself for the final act.

It was a dance of love, hot and wild and exciting. Val's legs clamped around Rush as she met each powerful thrust of his hips. Her heartbeat thundered in her chest, in her throat, her ears. They snatched breathy, gasping kisses, and groped greedily for whatever they could reach of each other.

Val had never felt such emotion before, not even during their first time in Rush's condo. She felt helpless and powerful at the same time, both a follower and a leader. Rush's strength and potency were overwhelming, but so were her own. What remained startling was the hunger within her, a sensation that kept growing and seemed to be enveloping the entire universe. She had not known her capacity for sexual need, and could only lay it on Rush.

Only seconds apart, they reached paradise, Val first, Rush immediately after. Their frenetic movements stilled, and the afterglow of fulfillment was almost as satisfying as the more volatile aspects of their lovemaking.

Val's eyes opened to stare at the ceiling. Rush's face was dug into the pillow next to her head. His skin was damp, as was hers, and her first distinct thought was of a cool, refreshing shower.

Her second wasn't nearly so mundane. There was so much wrong between them, and making love as though they were sex-starved and mindless changed nothing.

But when his head came up and she saw the warm, loving smile on his face, she altered that opinion. Making love at this particular time, in this particular place, changed a great deal. The first time could have been judged a chance occurrence, even, crudely, a one-night stand. This was different. This second episode smacked of commitment, of great significance, and from the look in Rush's eyes, he wasn't above pressing her for an advantage.

Val would never know why she said what she did, probably because something had to be done to shock that romantic look off Rush's face. "Should we run to the nearest preacher now, darling?"

He paled before her eyes. His smile disappeared. His mouth changed shapes. He puffed out air. "Uh . . . are you proposing?"

"It's a thought."

He cleared his throat. "But one that needs a little more . . . uh, thought."

"I figured you for far more impulsive."

"You're serious about . . . that preacher?"

If he wasn't so genuinely stricken, Val would have laughed. On the other hand, the subject wasn't particularly funny.

"May I get up?"

"Uh . . . sure. Yes. Of course." Rush moved to the bed, shaken by Val's introduction of marriage into their relationship. Did she mean it? He stared at the ceiling while she slid from the bed and went into the adjoining bathroom. Damn, he hadn't reacted very well. But her remark had taken him completely by surprise. Surely she didn't mean it. Maybe it had been some sort of test.

His eyes narrowed thoughtfully. What if she had meant it? Didn't a bid for marriage go along with high-necked dresses and an almost prudish outlook on life? Wouldn't an old-fashioned woman prefer marriage over an affair any day of the week?

He realized he was back to thinking of Val as charmingly outdated and, yes, he cared for her. A lot, to be honest. But marriage? Was he ready for the big step?

Rush got off the bed. He might be plenty ready, but he couldn't plunge into something that big and far-reaching without putting in some time on the idea. Val would understand, especially when he told her how much she had come to mean to him.

She returned to the bedroom, fully dressed. Rush was in the process of buttoning his shirt. He smiled. She smiled. Everything seemed fine.

Val went to the bureau for her purse. She picked up her hairpins and dropped them into the bag. "Dinner?" Rush said lightly, from behind her.

"Let me be frank, all right?" Val turned. "I'm exhausted, and my only goal right now is to go home, have a bath, a bite of supper and an early bedtime."

Rush's face fell. "Well, sure, if that's what you want."

"It is," Val said quietly. "See you tomorrow, okay?"

"Hey, don't run off so fast." Rush finished buckling his belt and strode across the room. With his hands on her waist, he tugged her forward. His eyes searched hers. "Did you mean what you said?"

Val's eyes widened. "Rush! Of course not. I was only kidding."

He tried hard to smile, but it came off pretty weak. "You're the most confusing woman I've ever known. Val, do you care anything at all about me?"

She touched his face and looked at him for the longest time. Finally she spoke. "Yes, Rush, I care about you. I can't explain myself today, but...I will." Her contract with the Casbah's production company required a three-week notice for leaving the show. The Saxon Springs project looked relatively secure now; her commissions would be coming in very soon. It was time to implement her long-range plan, and to make that final break with the entertainment world.

Rush wondered if he was hearing her right. "You will? When?" He'd spoken brusquely and dropped his hands from her waist. He ran his fingers through his hair. "Tell me about it right now, Val. Whatever it is, I can take it."

"But maybe I can't," she said unsteadily, which was the awful truth. She simply could not look Rush in the eye and describe Valentine, or attempt to justify what was bound to sound like deception, not while it was still going on. She was feeling like a sneak as it was, lying to him, evading his questions, putting on an act that was harder to do everyday. In three weeks, when there was no longer a secret to keep, she would tell him everything.

Val sighed. Until Rush came into her life, she'd seen her decision to separate her overlapping careers as wise and possibly even brilliant. Now she second-guessed her every move and had to watch every word that came out of her mouth.

The one thing she wasn't able to control was her over-powering physical attraction to Rush. It meant something, too. She didn't sleep around willy-nilly, and never had.

"Let me say something," she said quietly. "Until you, I never went to bed with a man I knew only two weeks." She saw Rush's wince and interpreted it, correctly, as a reaction to her mentioning other men. She arched an eyebrow. "Can you say the same about the women you've known?"

He shoved his hands into his pockets and looked stubborn. "Can you?" Val repeated with a touch of acerbity.

"No, but..."

"Let's not get into 'buts,' okay, Rush? We're grown-ups, reasonably intelligent people. You have to know I wasn't a virgin, and it certainly never entered my mind you might be that pure."

"You're saying to leave the past in the past. That's well and good, but what about the present?"

She sighed again. "Maybe the present will take care of it-self if you give it a chance. I'm only asking for a little time, Rush. Can't you be patient for a while longer?"

He turned his head and gave a sharp, disbelieving laugh. "Guess I don't have any choice."

Yet a third sigh lifted Val's shoulders. "Maybe I don't, either. I'm going now. See you tomorrow?"

"Yeah, tomorrow," he agreed halfheartedly. Then, as she disappeared from his sight, he yelled, "I'll never understand you if I live to be a hundred and fifty!"

Val's steps slowed. It was quite possible she didn't understand Val LeClair, either.

She resumed a normal pace to the front door. Whatever misunderstanding she had with herself, it hadn't started until Rush Saxon invaded her territory.

Nine

———

Thomas Delaney was an old friend of Val's. That is to say, she'd known him for a long time. Tom was about thirty-five, Val figured, so he was hardly old, certainly no more than five years her senior.

The Delaneys had lived down the block from the Le-Clairs during Val's adolescent years, on Minnow Street, and Tom's parents had often included Val's mother in neighborhood gatherings. Tom had been just enough older than Val to treat her as a kid sister, and he'd teased her to blushes many times.

They lost track of each other after Tom left home, and even more so when the elder Delaneys moved away from Minnow Street. Val was floored to see him walk into the sales office around eleven-thirty on Monday morning. At first she wasn't positive it was him. He was bigger, fleshier, and the marvelous head of hair he'd been so proud of in his youth had thinned significantly.

When he smiled his big brash smile and said hello, though, she greeted him with her hand out. "Tom Delaney, I believe."

He looked her up and down over the handshake, then enlightenment broadened his smile. "Valentine LeClair! Well, I'll be damned. It's been ... how long?"

"A very long time," she replied with a laugh. "How are you?"

"Thirty pounds heavier, as you can see." Tom patted the top of his head. "And a little lighter up here."

They laughed together. "Are you house-hunting?" Val asked.

"Not for myself, no. Are you the agent for this development?"

"That I am."

"But I thought I heard something about you dancing in some big show on the Strip."

"Um..." Val knew they were alone, but she looked around anyway and laughed self-consciously. "The owner of this project doesn't know about that, Tom. Would you mind not saying anything about it if he should happen to come in? Just call me Val, okay?"

"Whatever you say. It's none of my business." Tom flashed another smile. "Hey, this is great. How've you been?"

"Can't complain. And you?"

"Couldn't be better. I'm married to a great gal, by the way. Been married for eight years."

"Good for you. How are your parents?"

"They're reasonably well, and living in Arizona, Valentine. Oops, I mean, Val. How's your mother?"

"Mom died fourteen months ago, Tom."

He became sympathetic. "I'm sorry to hear that. I always liked her."

"Thank you." Val shaped a smile. "Well, if you're not house-hunting, what brings you to Saxon Springs?"

"Well, it's like this. I've got a nice piece of property just outside of Palm Springs, and I'm looking for someone who might be interested in developing it into residential housing. A friend told me to take a look at this project, since it's similar to what I've got in mind."

"Do you live in Palm Springs?"

"Off and on. Pam—that's my wife—and I have a house there, but we also have one here." Tom laughed. "Got one in McCall, Idaho, too, so when the heat gets us down, we head for the mountains. Pam's up there now."

Obviously Tom Delaney had done all right, Val thought. His affluence didn't surprise her; Tom always had been a go-getter. "Why don't we sit down?" She indicated the chairs around her desk.

"Sure," Tom agreed. "Thanks."

Settling behind the desk, Val regretted her dowdy appearance. Tom had to remember her flamboyant hairstyles and preference for colorful clothing when they were neighbors, and it was a trifle daunting to run into an old friend while knowing she could look much better than she did.

"So when did you get into real estate?" Tom questioned.

"About a year ago. I'm giving up dancing, Tom." Val smiled. "In fact, I gave the production manager my three-week notice just this morning."

"You're doing this on purpose, aren't you? The funny hairdo and flat heels, I mean?"

Val couldn't help laughing. "You're just the same, Tom, right to the point. But, yes, I'm doing it on purpose."

He leaned back and grinned. "Tell me about the owner of this project."

"What would you like to know?"

"Do you think he'd be interested in forming a partnership to develop my Palm Springs property?"

Val's first instinct said, no, but she couldn't state any such judgment to Tom. "I can't speak for Rush Saxon, Tom." She smiled. "But I could introduce you." In the very next instant she regretted speaking so hastily. Getting Tom Delaney and Rush together right now might not be best for her goals. If Tom should slip and say something about her musical career, she might find herself stumbling through an explanation weeks before she felt ready to cope with it.

But it was too late. Tom was nodding and beaming. "Is Saxon around the project today? I drove through it, and it seems to be coming along very well."

Somewhat discomfited by the topic, Val smoothed back a straying strand of hair from her cheek. There were an enormous amount of negative details about the project that could undermine Tom's interest. By the same token, Rush had taken charge admirably, and shouldn't be judged on the many missteps made before his arrival.

It was wisest for her to stay out of it completely, she decided. Rush could explain whatever he wanted Tom to know, if he was interested enough in the deal to go that far.

Still, it was a relief for Val to inform Tom that Rush was absent this morning. "We're in the process of closing some of the unit sales, and Rush had to sign papers at several different title companies."

Tom reached into his shirt pocket for a business card, which he passed to Val. "I'm sure he's a busy man. Ask him to give me a call when he has a few minutes."

Val tucked the card into her purse. "Be glad to."

Tom got to his feet. "Hey, how about letting an old friend take you to lunch? Can you leave for an hour or so?"

"Yes," Val said adamantly as she stood up. "It's been slow today, and I'd love to have lunch with you."

"Great."

"It'll take me a few minutes to lock the models."

"I'll come with you. I'd like to see the interior of these units."

"Certainly."

Val attempted a quick tour, preferring to leave before Rush showed up. But Tom took his time and inspected the closets, the cabinetry and the overall layout of each model.

"I'm impressed, Val. These are exactly the type of homes I have in mind for my Palm Springs property. The price range is right, too, though I'm pretty sure we could get twenty to forty thousand more for each unit in California."

"That would certainly increase your project's profit potential," Val observed.

"Yes, but don't forget that the cost of land is higher in the Palm Springs area than it is in Vegas. Land values in Southern Nevada have gone up in the last five or six years, but nothing like what's happened in Palm Springs."

"I'm sure that's true," Val agreed. She looked at her watch. "Well, I'm hungry. How about you?"

Tom nodded. "Let's go. Thanks for showing me around."

Val quickly locked up and led Tom through the sales office, which she locked, as well. They were settling into the front seat of his splendid BMW when she spotted Rush's car driving in. With enormous relief, she saw the vehicle make a turn and stop in front of one of the houses nearing completion, which put about half a block of distance between them.

Tom started the BMW's engine. Val furtively kept an eye on Rush, who got out of his car and headed into the house. She relaxed then and smiled at Tom, who leaned over and unexpectedly kissed her on the cheek. "This is great, Val. The minute Pam gets back to town, you two have to meet."

Actually Rush hadn't gone straight into the house, but paused to admire the sleek, silver BMW near the sales office. It nearly floored him to recognize Val in the passenger's seat, and the driver kissing her. At least, that was what he thought he saw. He blinked and then frowned. If the woman wasn't Val, she looked an awful lot like her from this distance.

Val's car was parked in its usual spot. Rush's plans changed immediately, and he ran back to his car, hopped in without bothering with the door and drove to the sales office. The BMW pulled onto the street and disappeared in traffic. Rush jumped out of his car and loped to the door of the building. Finding it locked, he turned to stare grimly at the string of unfamiliar vehicles passing the project.

He'd seen exactly what he'd thought; Val had left with some guy, a guy who was friendly enough to kiss her in broad daylight in front of her place of business.

Rush's mouth tightened to a thin, tense line. What the hell kind of fool was he? She'd said there was no other man, but there he was, picking her up in his fancy car, kissing her, taking her...where? The proof was Rush's own eyesight. How many kinds of sap could a man be? He felt crushed, betrayed and his mind was a blank about what he should do about it.

The hot sun broiled down from a cloudless hot sky. When the heat finally registered, Rush unlocked the office door with his key and went inside. He got himself a glass of water and gulped it without a breath, then sat at his desk with a vacant stare.

No more, he thought when his brain started functioning again. He'd done everything but turn handsprings for Val, and he'd behaved like a lovesick schoolboy long enough. This was the end of it.

Feeling numb, Rush got up, went through the outside door, made sure it was locked and walked to his car. He had driven several miles when he realized he had no destination.

He kept on going.

Val enjoyed her lunch with Tom. They reminisced about their parents and Minnow Street, and he told her more about Pam. "We wanted children right away, but none came along. We're working on adoption now."

"And you've done well financially. I'm glad, Tom."

"Mostly in real estate, Val. It's a good field for an enterprising person. I started out much as you're doing, with a license to sell and little else besides ambition and determination. I gave up my license a few years back, because I'm as busy as I want to be with my own properties."

Tom's success was thrilling for Val, indicating a secure future for anyone who went after it. That was what she wanted, almost desperately. Certainly she had the ambition and determination Tom mentioned. Her show business career had been satisfying for years, but she had grown beyond it and was looking to the future.

They had eaten in a small restaurant known for its excellent stir-fry menu, and in Val's estimation, the food had been as good as the company. She had liked Tom Delaney when he'd been a young man full of teasing good nature, and she liked him now.

Tom drove her back to the project, chatting all the way about Pam and Val meeting at the first opportunity. "I go back and forth during the summer, but Pam stays in McCall during July and August. Our house is right on the lake, and she just can't tear herself away from those cool breezes when it's a hundred and ten down here."

"I don't blame her." The BMW stopped in front of the sales office. Rush's car was nowhere in sight. "This has been wonderful, Tom. Thank you."

"We'll do it again. Be sure to give Mr. Saxon my card."

"I will." Smiling, Val got out. She waved at Tom as he drove off, then unlocked the door to the sales office and went in.

She felt good. Tom showing up had been a marvelous surprise. Humming under her breath, Val went to unlock the models.

Val's second surprise of the day was Rush's absence. He was always in and out of the sales office, but after that one visit to the project around noon, he must have gone off and not returned. Odd.

Still, she was too busy to dwell on what Rush might be doing. People straggled in all afternoon, and one couple put money down on a house, which made the day a success in Val's book.

Her earned commissions were adding up to an impressive sum. She had worked hard, and not too many agents would take on a project of this size all by themselves. Her time off had been practically nil for months and months, especially when she also worked five nights of every week.

But as Tom had pointed out, it took ambition and determination to attain success. And when her commission checks started rolling in, she would be able to pay the balances due on those medical bills, which would be an incredible reduction of her fiscal responsibility. Val honestly didn't know how it felt to be without debt, and lots of it.

It was almost over. She could see the light at the end of the tunnel. It was Rush's doing, of course. If he hadn't arrived on the scene when he did, and saved the project from certain death, all her hard work would have amounted to nothing. She owed Rush a great deal of gratitude, and maybe she'd been remiss in letting him know.

It was an easily rectified oversight, Val thought, one she would take care of the very next time she saw him.

At four, however, he still hadn't shown up, and Val locked the models by herself. She drove past the Saxon company office, thinking he might be there, but only saw vacant parking spaces.

At home, she showered, puttered around the kitchen for a while, and with a growing unease, dialed Larry's condo. There was no answer, and her unease turned to foreboding.

Silly, she called herself, scoffing at her imagination as she put down the phone. Why would she think something was wrong just because Rush hadn't been underfoot all day? Did she wish he'd shown up at four to chase her around the models again?

The evening passed slowly. Val ate a light supper, and as darkness descended she went to the pool. No one was there. She swam laps until she was exhausted and then went home.

Wearing her nightgown and robe, she eyed the telephone. A good excuse to speak to Rush was in her purse: Tom's business card.

But she wasn't completely sold on the two men getting together. Still, it wasn't her decision to make. She had agreed to giving Rush the card and asking him to call Tom. With a frown of uncertainty, she picked up the phone and heard a brusque "Hello" after two rings.

"Oh, you're home."

"Val?"

"Yes. I called earlier, but there was no answer."

"I just now walked in."

There was something distinctly different about his voice, an unfamiliar coolness. It made Val feel as though she were intruding, which had never before happened with Rush.

"I have a message for you. A business card, actually."

"From whom?"

"A man by the name of Tom Delaney came by the project today. He owns property near Palm Springs and is looking for a partner to develop it. He looked at Saxon Springs and likes what you're doing, and requested that you give him a call. If you're interested in his offer, that is," she added after a brief pause.

"I might be. You have his card, you said?"

"Yes."

"Bring it with you in the morning."

"Oh. Well, fine. Yes, I'll do that. Uh, Rush, is everything all right?"

"Why wouldn't it be?"

"No reason, I guess. You just sound sort of... distant."

The chill factor in Rush's voice dropped another degree. "Aren't you going out tonight?"

"Why... no," Val replied, slowly. Her mind was working a little faster. Maybe he wanted to come over, or invite her to his place. What would she say to either invitation? They would make love again, and they shouldn't. Each incident of intimacy brought them emotionally closer, and it wasn't fair to Rush when there was so much about her he didn't know yet.

"Well, get a good night's sleep," Rush drawled. "See you in the morning."

Val's eyes widened with shock when Rush's phone clicked in her ear. She put her own phone down with an expression of disbelief. Something *was* wrong, terribly wrong. Only yesterday Rush would have pressed her for a meeting, and tonight he was barely civil.

Stewing over it didn't help, but Val couldn't change the direction of her thoughts. Rush had become very important very quickly, and his about-face was startling and unnerving. Why would he suddenly turn off on her?

But maybe it hadn't been that sudden. He'd been upset yesterday when she left him in the bedroom of the model, and she probably should have taken his mood more seriously than she had.

Was there a way to undo whatever damage had been done yesterday? For the first time since Rush came barging into her life, Val worried about the evolution of their personal relationship. She was as close to falling in love as she'd ever been, and she didn't want it to come to a screeching halt over nothing.

Well, it hadn't been nothing, but neither should a simple request for a little time and patience from Rush cause this. Val didn't usually function on impulse, but she suddenly dug into her purse for Tom's card and dashed out into the night.

She was well away from her condo when she remembered her bare feet and nightclothes. They were of no consequence, she thought as she hurried along the sidewalk. At Larry's condo, which was dark, she rang the doorbell, leaning on it with her thumb so it pealed for a good long time.

Rush got out of bed, rather grumpily, dragged on pants, snapped on lights as he went, and finally jerked the door open. "Yes? Oh, it's you."

"I . . . brought this." Val held out the card.

"I told you it could wait till morning." She was speechless. A cooler reception she'd never received from anyone. Rush took the card. "Thanks."

"You're welcome." Val squirmed. He was only half-dressed. Or rather, he was half-naked. "Sorry if I got you out of bed. It isn't that late, and..."

"Yeah, well, I was tired. I *am* tired." He looked her in the eye. "Like you were last night."

She tried to laugh. "You're angry about something, aren't you?"

"Not in the least. I put in a long day and I'm tired." His gaze remained locked with hers. "Anything else?"

She took a shaky breath and dropped her eyes. "No. I just thought you might want...that card."

Rush nearly relented. She looked beautiful standing in the lights from the condo. Her hair was flying every which way, just the way he liked it, and her clothing was a robe, something pink and pretty. The prettiest garment he'd ever seen her wearing, in fact.

But then his spine stiffened. He was tired of playing her game, and if Val needed two men to be happy, she'd have to look elsewhere. He wasn't going to be one of them.

"Good night," he said gruffly.

"Uh...good night." Val backed up and turned to go, wondering if he would have closed the door in her face if she hadn't given ground. As it was, he'd shut it awfully fast, as though he couldn't stand the sight of her.

Her legs shook during the hike back to her own place, and she went in fighting tears. The shoe was definitely on the other foot now, she unhappily realized. Instead of Rush pursuing her and her backing off, *he* was backing off and she wanted him.

With her fingertips pressed to her trembling lips, Val curled up on the sofa in her living room. In God's name, why? What had happened between last night and tonight to turn everything upside down? She remembered him shouting, "I'll never understand you if I live to be a hundred and fifty!'' and wished that she had gone back and talked to him instead of leaving. What if this was truly the end? Could she bear it?

The future looked bleak. Having her bills paid wouldn't make up for losing Rush. She had carried her charade too far, protected her privacy too long. She should have told him everything right away, and certainly when he began pressuring her about her mystique.

An hour later, exhausted from crying and worrying, Val got up and stumbled to her bedroom. She had to see the Saxon Springs project through to the bitter end, which meant working with Rush however uncomfortable they might be. Time changed all things, and if he ever gave her the chance to explain, she would do it in a heartbeat.

Somehow she knew that wasn't going to happen: Rush had written her off.

Ten

___

Rush had a long conversation with Tom Delaney on the phone the next morning, and liked him. Tom was friendly, easy to talk to and promoting what seemed to be a sound business proposition, the development of his Palm Springs property. He outlined his business background for Rush, then told him about the land specifically and the Palm Springs area in general. "I like your Saxon Springs project, Rush. It's almost exactly what I have in mind for my property."

"I'm interested, Tom." It surprised Rush just how interested he really was. He was so interested, in fact, he was hesitant to tell Tom how new he was to the business world. Obviously Tom thought otherwise, and Rush found himself skirting the subject.

"I'd like you to take a look at the property, Rush. We could fly down, or drive. It's only a four-hour trip by car."

"I'd like to see it," Rush agreed, but wondered if he would understand what he was seeing. He needed a more

expert opinion than his own, and the only expert he knew in
the field of real estate was Val. Granted, she was almost as
new to the business as he was, but she was bright and savvy,
and he didn't like the idea of bringing a completely unknown person into a deal that was just barely getting
started. Later, if needed, he could locate and hire an ac-
credited land appraiser. Val might even know of one.

"Tom, I should be in a position to view your property by
the end of the week. Would this coming weekend fit your
schedule?" Convincing Val to accompany him might take
some doing, considering their present relationship. They
spoke, of course, they had to. But Rush's personal with-
drawal was obvious, and he could see questions in Val's eyes
every time they were together, which annoyed him, as he
couldn't believe she didn't have some understanding of the
situation.

"This weekend would be fine, Rush. Anytime, actually,
but the sooner the better."

"Would you mind if I brought someone else along?"

"Not at all. Bring anyone you wish."

Rush didn't explain about who he had in mind, and Tom
didn't ask. They signed off with tentative plans to drive to
Palm Springs during the weekend.

Rush brought up the subject to Val later in the day, doing so with a casually stated "I talked to Tom Delaney."

"Oh?" Val looked up from the work on her desk, surprised but pleased that Rush was instigating an unnecessary conversation. She'd been trying to work but too often
she caught herself daydreaming. Not about a secure future,
as she used to, but about Rush and how strangely he was
acting. He was indifferent now, and it hurt and puzzled her.

"He wants me to take a look at his land in Palm Springs."

Val sat back. "Then you're interested in his plans for the
property?"

Rush frowned slightly. "Do you know his plans?"

"He mentioned them. The day he left his card for you."

"Chatty, was he?" Rush's thoughts focused on his own omissions with Tom. "And what did you tell him?"

"I beg your pardon?"

"About me."

Val blinked. "I certainly didn't say anything derogatory about you, if that's what you're thinking." Was that what was bothering Rush? The possibility of her talking to Tom about him? Pushing back her chair, Val stood up. "Rush, there was very little said about you that day. Your name was mentioned only in the context of this project."

"Delaney didn't ask about my background?"

"Of course not." Val was beginning to glimpse the reason behind Rush's questions. "Rest assured," she said quietly. "Any information I might pick up in the course of our business relationship is strictly confidential."

Realizing he had reached a conclusion much too hastily, Rush felt a little foolish. "Sorry," he said. "It's just that..." From Val's expression, she fully grasped the machinations of his thoughts, and embarrassment heightened his color. He let the subject drop, and said instead, "Would you consider going along?"

"Go? To Palm Springs, you mean? Uh...may I know why?" Val was afraid to think the idea had personal implications, but what else could it be? Their relationship was so blasted complex, and there were things about Rush she didn't comprehend, just as he didn't understand her. But why else would he ask her to go with him, if not to be together? Val's heart began beating faster with an undeniable joy.

"Because I need your expertise," Rush said evenly.

"My what?"

"Your knowledge of real estate."

Deflated, Val sank back to her chair. "My knowledge of real estate is extremely limited. Your thinking I'm some kind of expert in the field is almost laughable," she said dully. "And what I know about the Palm Springs area wouldn't cover the head of a pin."

"I don't want to bring in a stranger. Later on, if the deal looks promising, but not yet."

"I'm not licensed in California."

"You don't need a license to form an opinion. That's all I'm asking for, a simple, one-two-three opinion."

Their opposing viewpoints hung in the air. Val's hope for more than a business liaison between them had died a crushing death. That phase of their relationship was truly over, and the agony in her system was almost unbearable.

But he would never know it. Val lifted her chin. "When are you going?"

"This weekend."

"I could be gone Sunday, Monday or both, but what about this project? We can't just close the doors."

"Yes, we can. I was thinking of Saturday and Sunday."

"Not Saturday," Val rebutted, repeating, "Sunday and Monday."

Rush experienced frustration, the same feeling he always got during conversations with Val. "Why not Saturday?"

She would never tell him the truth now, Val thought stubbornly and with no small amount of pain. He'd turned off on her without cause, and maybe her initial assessment of Rush was the most accurate: He was full of himself. And inconsiderate.

"I'm busy on Saturday night," she said flatly.

Instant anger tensed Rush's jaw. She probably had a date with that joker who'd been driving the BMW. "Are your plans so important you can't change them?"

"Are yours?" she shot back.

His plans were flexible, but Val's attitude was infuriating. "Fine," he snapped hotly. "We'll make it Sunday or Monday. We certainly wouldn't want to interfere with your love life, would we?"

"My...?" Val's mouth hung open. "What on earth are you talking about?"

Rush was steaming, and he honestly feared what might come out of his mouth in this mood. "Let's just drop it, okay? I've got work to do. See you later.'' He walked to the door and yanked it open.

Val stared, stunned to speechlessness, as Rush went outside and stalked to his car. He wasn't convinced there was no other man in her life, and he was furious about it. Why would he care, if he didn't feel something for her?

She got weak from the significance of Rush's anger. It *wasn't* over between them, so why was he behaving so coldly if he still felt something for her? His change of heart had happened so quickly, without warning. Something she wasn't aware of had taken place, but what?

Val became very still. Had Tom said something about her stage career during his and Rush's telephone conversation?

But, no, Rush had become distant before that. Besides, he was back to thinking her involved evenings were because of a man. Because of her love life.

She had to tell him the truth, Val thought unhappily. However Rush ultimately saw her double life, her evasiveness was destroying any chance they had.

And she wanted a chance, desperately. It wasn't possible to avoid her own feelings any longer: She was in love with Rush, and probably would be until her dying day.

The very next time she saw him, he was going to hear the whole story, every word of it. All she could do in the meantime was pray that he wouldn't take her transition from staid real estate agent to showgirl as a personal blow to his male pride.

Val couldn't tell if Rush was doing it deliberately, but she never had one moment alone with him during the ensuing days. He never came into the sales office unless she was busy with customers, and even when she remarked, several times, that she needed to speak to him privately, he never engineered an opportunity to do so.

She called him at home in the evenings before she left for the Casbah, and he never answered. She drove by the company office during the day, and he was never there. He was spending a lot of time on the construction site, she knew, but when he wasn't there, she had no idea where to find him.

The trip to Palm Springs became meaningful, a milestone. There would be hours together during the drive, and she practiced her story in her mind, repeatedly, to be ready for it, until Rush popped in one afternoon and told her when the sales office was full of clients and she couldn't expand the subject, that they would be riding with Tom Delaney.

By Saturday night Val was a bundle of nerves. The thought of Tom making a slip and Rush figuring out everything from that instead of hearing it from her, was frightening. For the first time in this fiasco, she felt deceitful, as though she had deliberately set out to sway Rush's opinion of her. She kept remembering that it was the woman she portrayed herself to be who had attracted him, and not a half-nude dancer performing on stage with dozens of other half-nude dancers.

Actually the professional dancers in the show were not even seminude, though their dazzling costumes left little to the imagination. But Val had seen just as much bare skin on television variety shows labeled family fare, and the volatile, energetic routines she and the other cast members executed five nights a week would be difficult if not impossible with ordinary clothing.

Near-nudity wasn't her problem with Rush. Neither was performing, in general. What nagged at her was how Rush saw her now, and how he might take hearing she hadn't been honest with him.

After the Saturday night show, Val quickly removed her stage makeup and prepared to leave. "We're going out to eat," one of the girls told her. "Why don't you come with us, like you used to?"

Neglecting longtime friends was one of the penalties of holding down two jobs, Val thought wryly. "Thanks," she said. "But I have to be up early."

She went home to her usual tea and toast, only to find little comfort in the ritual. Neither could she get to sleep, and when her alarm rang at 6:00 a.m., she could hardly drag herself out of bed.

Rush's doorbell chimed at six sharp. He opened the door with a smile, glad to finally meet the man he'd been talking to all week by telephone. "Tom?" He held out his hand.

They shook hands, with Tom stating, "You're younger than I thought from your voice."

"Come on in. Val should be along any minute."

"Valen... *Val* is the person you're taking with us? Hey, that's great."

Rush led his guest to the kitchen and poured him a cup of coffee. Tom Delaney was easily his height, but heavier. A little older, maybe five or six years. A man with a pleasant face and a broad smile, a man he liked in person, just as he'd liked him on the phone.

Sipping his coffee, Tom looked around. "Nice condo."

"Thanks," Rush returned, neglecting to mention the place was a rental. "Val lives in this same complex." The doorbell chimed again. "There she is now. Bring your coffee, if you want, Tom. We may as well get going."

Val stood at the door, sleepy-eyed and carrying a pillow. "Good morning, Rush. Hello, Tom," she said with a rather wan smile. "Hope you two don't mind if I crash in the back seat during the drive."

Tom chuckled. "Not at all."

Rush frowned. "Up all night?"

"Most of it," Val admitted, too tired this morning to care how he might interpret her reply.

The three of them started down the walk. Rush stopped suddenly, frozen with shock. The BMW he'd seen at the sales office was parked at the curb, the same damned car! His startled gaze darted back and forth between Val and Tom, both of whom were heading for the infamous vehicle as unconcerned as anyone Rush had ever seen. Yet he'd witnessed with his own eyes Tom Delaney kissing Val that day. Whoa, he thought. What in hell was going on here?

"Rush?" Tom was at his car and looking back, grinning. "Forget something?"

Confusion gripped Rush. Was Tom Val's boyfriend or wasn't he? And if he was, why were the two of them acting like they barely knew each other?

Or was he missing something? With narrowed, suspicious eyes, Rush approached the BMW. Val crawled into the back seat, plumped her pillow against the far door and got herself comfortable against it. Tom climbed into the driver's seat, and Rush, shaken to his soul, finally settled onto the passenger's seat.

Cheerfully Tom remarked on the cool morning air as he drove from the complex. "Early morning is the best time of day in the desert, I always say."

Rush grunted out some sort of barely intelligible comment. His thoughts weren't on the weather or the time of day. Val and Tom couldn't have been together last night, not with her exhausted and him as fresh as an ocean breeze. But Rush knew what he'd seen that day, and Val had been in this car and Tom had kissed her.

Tom began talking about his Palm Springs property. Val tuned out the voices in the front seat and was soon fast asleep. About an hour out of Las Vegas, Rush sent a glance to the back seat and was relieved to see Val sleeping. He looked at Tom.

"Have you and Val known each other very long?" he questioned nonchalantly.

"Long time," Tom confirmed. "Fifteen years, at least."

"No kidding," Rush said flatly. "She didn't tell me that."

Tom shrugged. "She's got her hands full, what with working . . . I mean, she seems to be doing a good job with Saxon Springs."

"Yes, she is," Rush agreed, slowly. He kept checking Tom out, and he nearly swallowed his teeth when he spotted a gold ring on Tom's left hand. "Uh, Tom, is that a wedding ring you're wearing?"

Tom gave his ring a proud glance. "Married eight years now, Rush. Are you married?"

"No." Rush felt about six inches high. So much anger-inspired adrenaline had pumped through his system for the past hour and a half, he felt ill from it. Weak and ill. Why was he constantly jumping to conclusions with Val? The kiss he'd seen that had nearly destroyed him had been nothing more than a gesture from an old friend. Something was going on with Val, but that something wasn't Tom Delaney.

The plan was to look at the property and drive back to Las Vegas yet today. It would be a long day, but flying commercial would not have shortened it by much, and driving had valuable side benefits for Rush, such as Tom's commentary on the economics of the towns they passed through.

The Southwest was Rush's home now, a fact that was sinking in deeper by the day. He could chuck the whole idea and go somewhere else to make his living, but how smart would that be? As financially shaky as the Saxon Construction Company was, it was a darned good foothold in the business world. And once the unit sales began closing—very soon now—the company wouldn't be so shaky. Nor would he.

No, Rush thought. He wasn't going anywhere. He liked Vegas in spite of the summer heat, and the business opportunities were limited only by one's own ambition and imagination. His were soaring, an unexpected bonus in this strange chapter of his life. Tom Delaney's appearance and offer felt like a sign of good things to come. This deal might not reach fruition, but there would be others.

And there was Val. Rush glanced over his shoulder again. Val's hair was spread over the pillow beneath her head. It had been pinned back haphazardly, loosely, this morning, and he could see a fallen hairpin lying on Val's shoulder. Her face was serene in sleep, a beautiful face with high cheekbones and a flawless, creamy complexion. Val didn't need makeup to draw attention to herself, he thought, and she wasn't plain because of it, either. How could he ever have thought she was? She was special, unique, head and shoulders above any woman he'd ever known. He loved her.

A frisson of pure energy danced up Rush's spine. He loved Val LeClair. It was the most solid, immutable feeling he'd ever possessed. He loved her, and he'd done little but doubt her. Was that the way of a man falling in love? To doubt and challenge what was happening to him?

Whatever Val's secret was—and she had one, make no mistake—it had nothing to do with him. If it did, Val would have told him about it. That she hadn't indicated a problem she intended to solve by herself and a courage he should admire. She was a valiant lady, and instead of poking and prying, and demanding more than she could give, he should be grateful for her spirit of independence and respectful of her tenacity.

He would be from now on. No more questions, he told himself. He wanted Val in his life, in his future, and he'd been driving her away with his ridiculous suspicions.

They reached the city of Palm Springs a little before eleven. As Rush had never been there, Tom drove around to give him a taste of the area. Val woke up slowly, becoming gradually aware of the lesser speed of the car and the sounds of city traffic.

She raised her lashes to see Rush looking at her. He gave her a smile that reached his eyes and set her pulse to racing, the kind of smile she had seen on his handsome face prior to the last few days.

"Feeling better?" he asked softly.

Val was almost lying down on the seat, and she lay there and let the silent signals pass back and forth between them. It was a delicious moment, rife with sexual innuendo and warm emotions. But even while enjoying it, Val wondered about Rush's changeability. One minute he was cold with

her, the next hot, and the cause of his mood swings alway
escaped her.

"Much better," she replied, pulling herself upright. "
slept the entire trip!" she exclaimed as she recognized where
they were.

Tom knew the city well, and he drove them through the
downtown area with its splendid shops, and then past lusk
golf courses and incredibly beautiful residential areas. "Thi
is where my house is located," he said while turning onto a
street lined with large elegant homes and palm trees. "How
about some lunch before we drive out to the property?"

Val immediately voted yes, as she had stumbled out of bed
in a fog and hadn't eaten that morning. Rush agreed with
thanks, and Tom pulled into the driveway of a gorgeous
white stucco house. He raised the garage door with a re
mote control and parked the BMW.

Rush got out quickly and opened the door for Val, who
exited while picking up very warm vibes from him. It was an
exciting sensation, but she still wondered what had altered
his attitude so drastically.

The housekeeper, Mary, greeted them, and after intro
ductions, Tom requested lunch. Rush felt right at home
Before Las Vegas, this was what he'd been accustomed to
elegant surroundings and pleasant servants doing his bid
ding.

But Val wasn't, and she was impressed by Tom's obvious
affluence, particularly since he also had a home in Las Ve
gas and another in McCall, Idaho.

Tom showed his guests to the bathrooms, bringing Val to
the master suite. "This bathroom is Pam's," he told her
"Use whatever you might need in the way of lotions or what
have you. Pam won't mind."

Val was awake but still a little groggy. "Thank you,
Tom." Alone, she washed her face and brushed her hair.
The bathroom was white and gold, stunningly beautiful and
equipped with everything from hand lotion to lipstick.

But she didn't need to borrow from Pam Delaney. Val dug out the cosmetics she had thrown into her purse on impulse, and carefully did her face, using color subtly and sparingly. Instead of pinning her hair back, she fluffed it around her face then swept it back with two pretty combs. Her clothing was a simple white skirt and pink-and-white blouse, and couldn't be changed. But she unbuttoned the top two buttons of her blouse and rolled up her sleeves. A touch of perfume completed her preparations.

Val felt a deep inner excitement and no small amount of dread. Not having the facility to understand Rush's moods didn't reduce her feelings for him, and something told Val that an opportunity was going to arise during this trip to speak to him privately. She was going to tell him everything, and looking better than she normally did around him gave her some much-needed confidence.

She left the bathroom and found the two men seated in the living room. They stood up. Rush stared. Tom said, "Sit down, Val." She sat. Tom resumed his seat. Rush stood there and stared.

Then he realized what he was doing and sat down with a small frown. Val's pulse fluttered. Didn't he like her with makeup and her hair this way?

They chatted about this and that until Mary announced lunch was ready, then got up and went to the dining room to dine on a delicious chicken salad and crusty French bread. Halfway through lunch, Tom got a phone call. Excusing himself, he left the room.

Rush put down his fork and regarded Val across the table, speaking very quietly. "You're so beautiful, you take my breath." He wanted to ask why she was wearing makeup today, when she never did. The questions kept piling up with Val, but he vowed to bite off his tongue before asking them. That phase of their relationship was over. He would never mistrust her or her motives again.

"Thank you," she replied in a rather frantic whisper. "Rush, I need to talk to you. When we're alone." Her pulse beat erratically at the mere thought of speaking so frankly, but it had to be done.

"I need to talk to you, too." He was nearly bursting with the things he wanted to say to her, apologies, definitely, and it was time she learned how important she had become to him. He wanted more than conversation with Val, though. He wanted to finish unbuttoning that blouse, and lift her skirt, undress her, feel her body against his, under his, her mouth on his.

His desire was in his eyes. Val's heart skipped a beat, because his thoughts were so readable. "What happened?" she whispered. "Yesterday you were so..."

Tom walked in and took his place at the table. "I need to ask a favor. Do either of you have to get back to Vegas tonight? There's a man in town I've been trying to see for some time. That was him on the phone, and he's free to meet me tonight if I can stay over. Would you mind staying and driving back first thing in the morning?"

Rush looked at Val. "It's all right with me, Tom."

Val nodded. That opportunity she'd been hoping for was suddenly within reach. "I can stay."

"You're sure it won't put you out?"

Rush nodded. "I'm sure, Tom. Besides, if we needed to get back, we could fly. Don't worry about it. A night in this beautiful house is certainly no hardship."

"I really appreciate your attitude, Rush. Thanks, Val."

"No problem," she said with a small, uncertain smile. Tonight, while Tom kept his appointment, she and Rush would be alone. They would have that belated discussion.

Their relationship could go no further without it.

Eleven

Tom's property looked like a chunk of barren desert to Rush, just as every other piece of vacant land did around Palm Springs. But the street was paved and the utilities—water, electricity, gas and sewer—were already on the property, a major consideration in development.

It was obvious that Tom Delaney wasn't a poor man, which raised Rush's curiosity. "I have to ask, Tom. Why are you looking for a partner?"

Tom was candid. "I usually avoid partnerships, Rush, but this development is a little more complex than anything I've done yet. I need someone like yourself who's already been through the mill. Your Saxon Springs is a terrific project. The house plans are livable and affordable. I'm planning a working man's development, Rush, which this area needs, and I'd like to use your blueprints and layouts, almost exactly as they are. We'd have to get them approved in California and by the county, of course. There's an enormous amount of red tape to wade through to build anything in this

state, but I'm sure you ran into some of the same bureau-
cracy in Nevada.''

They were braving the sweltering sun to walk a portion of
the arid ground, and Val was only a few feet away. Rush saw
her turn and look at him, as though awaiting his reply to
Tom's assumption.

Rush cleared his throat. "Are you planning to sell the
project yourself, Tom?"

"I'll probably do what you did, hire a darned good real
estate agent," Tom said with a laugh and an admiring glance
at Val.

The moment passed, but Val realized that Rush wasn't
being completely up-front with Tom. Maybe it wasn't important, she cautioned herself. Rush was intelligent and a
fast learner, and she didn't doubt his integrity when it came
to money. If he and Tom reached an agreement, Rush would
do his best to live up to it.

Still, Rush's omission proved him to be less than perfect.
His imperfections were very close to her own, for that matter. An omission wasn't really a lie, was it? Wasn't that an
argument for her own behavior?

Tom kept them occupied all afternoon. They visited other
development sites for comparisons, and picked up brochures. Tom introduced them to so many people, construction workers as well as project managers, Val lost track of
names and faces.

One thing was certain: She liked Tom's plans for his land,
and as she trusted both men as far as business went, she felt
a partnership would be beneficial to each. There was one
point she noticed and deemed important: Tom's property
was larger and would accommodate many more units than
the Saxon Springs project.

They returned to Tom's home around six. "Take a
shower, if you'd like," he told them. "That's what I'm going to do. Then we'll have a drink before enjoying one of
Mary's good dinners. By the way, Val, Pam's about your
size and there's a closet full of clothes in the master suite.

Feel free to help yourself. I'll get some clean clothes from my closet and use another bathroom. Rush, you're welcome to any of my things. I've got some athletic garb that might not slide off of you."

The men went off laughing, and Val waited until Tom came out of the master suite carrying fresh clothing.

"This is putting you out, Tom," she said reproachfully. "Let me use another room."

"Nope. You get the master suite tonight. No arguments, okay?"

Val couldn't see herself going through a strange woman's closet even if she was the wife of an old friend, but when she undressed for a shower, her own clothes were so sticky and wrinkled, the thought of putting them on again was unbearable. She would have to do so in the morning, of course, but something fresh for this evening would be greatly appreciated. Tom was going out of his way to be a gracious host, and she should take him at his word, Val finally decided. Hopefully Pam was as nice as he claimed, as most women would resent a stranger snooping through their things.

In the end, Val chose what appeared to be an inexpensive, washable caftan from Pam's stylish Palm Springs wardrobe. She rinsed out her underwear for morning and went without it for tonight, as the caftan was ample camouflage for a braless, pantyless figure.

When they congregated in the living room again, Rush was wearing a pair of white sweatpants and a blue T-shirt. The clothes were too large and hung on his lean frame in an adorable manner. Val raised an eyebrow, and Rush sent her a grin.

Tom fixed drinks and passed them around. They talked and sipped and spent an enjoyable half hour before dinner was announced, then went to the dining room and feasted on Mary's fine cooking.

Throughout the pleasant meal, Val was aware of Rush watching her, and could only hope that Tom didn't sense the same eagerness she did in Rush for their host to get on with his plans for the evening and leave them alone. It finally happened. Tom checked his watch at ten to eight and said he'd be late for his meeting if he didn't get going. On his way out, he warned them not to wait up for him as he might be late. A final message was that Mary would clean up, and they were to relax and enjoy the evening. Maybe take a swim in the pool in the backyard. There were suits available in the pool house, if they were so inclined.

With Tom's departure, the lovely dining room became silent. Val reached for her glass of iced tea and took a drink. Rush fidgeted with his napkin. They looked at each other across the table. It was, at long last, showdown time, and neither was all that confident, if for very diverse reasons.

But a burst of courage brought Val to her feet. "Where would you like to talk?"

"How about my room?" Rush smiled as he uncoiled his long body and stood up.

Val's mouth went dry. "The living room or outside by the pool would be far more sensible."

"It's too hot to sit outside, and the living room isn't exactly private."

They could hear Mary moving around the kitchen, but Val hadn't planned to hold this discussion anywhere near a bed. Still, there was an element in the air that seemed to be squeezing the oxygen out of her, something almost mysterious and certainly seductive. It probably had to do with being in someone else's house, and knowing there were things that had to be talked about when they would both much rather forget conversation altogether.

"Rush . . . please," she said huskily. "We really need to talk."

He came around the table. "We will. I promise. Do you know how beautiful you are tonight?" He stopped within inches of her. "And how much I want you?" he whispered. "I've been half crazy all day. Tom's meeting was a godsend, an answer to my prayers. Val, come to my room." He took her hands and began backing up, urging her forward, leading her from the dining room.

Val sent an uneasy glance to the door that she knew connected with the kitchen. "What about Mary?"

"I'm sure she doesn't give two hoots about how we might spend the evening."

"But you're thinking of..."

"Yes, I am," Rush affirmed. He leaned forward suddenly, putting his mouth to Val's ear to whisper, "I love you, baby. Let me show you how much."

A bolt of lightning couldn't have hit Val any harder. Her lips parted as her eyes widened, and her heart nearly burst in her chest. Dazed, she began following Rush's lead. Beyond the dining room, he put his arm around her shoulders and brought her to a beautiful bedroom decorated in pastel colors, softly lighted by two lamps with peach fabric shades.

Rush closed the door behind them. Val heard the click of the lock. Rush pulled her into his arms and kissed her until her legs trembled. She was gasping for breath when he raised his head and whispered, "Did you hear what I said in the dining room?"

She nodded weakly. "I think so. But I need to tell you something before..."

"You don't need to tell me anything, and certainly not before," he said raggedly, drawing her over to the bed. Quickly he yanked down the spread and top sheet.

Val was trying desperately to remember her vow to bare her soul. "Rush...listen to me...please..."

He was through arranging the bed and eager to use it. "Later, baby. We'll talk later," he growled.

In his arms again, Val's mind spun. He loved her, and he didn't know the truth yet. Dear God.

But his desire was inciting her own, and she kissed him back with as much hunger as his. His hands skimmed the long caftan covering her nudity, and in the next instant, so it seemed to a befuddled Val, the garment was unzipped and puddling on the floor around her ankles.

Rush sucked in a sharp breath. "If I'd known you had nothing on under that thing, I wouldn't have been able to sit still at that table and eat dinner." He pulled the T-shirt over his head and dropped his pants.

They fell to the bed, arms and legs tangling. Rush's hands wove into her hair as he whispered, "This is exciting. Val, you're so beautiful with makeup and your hair like this. I love you, baby. I knew something extraordinary was happening with us, but I didn't realize what it was until very recently."

Tears filled Val's eyes. "I love you, too."

"Show me, baby, show me." Rush moved on top of her. His face was taut with passion as he thrust into her heat.

Val let out a cry, but it was from pleasure and love, not from any discomfort. Their lovemaking was tumultuous, almost savage from their deeply aroused emotions. They took and took from each other, and gave without reservations or inhibitions, neither holding anything back.

Rush rolled them over, placing Val above him. He caressed her breasts and then brought her head down for breath-stealing kisses. Her hair tumbled around their faces, and he gloried in its smell, and twisted his fingers through it to savor its texture.

"Do you believe I love you?" he whispered hoarsely.

"Yes . . . yes."

"And you love me."

"I do. I love you," she gasped.

He turned them over again, placing Val on her back. "We're going to be together for the rest of our lives," he told her, his eyes dark and bottomless with emotion.

Val's eyes were swimming. In the back of her mind was that delayed conversation. It would be harder to do now . . . or would it be easier? Did he love her enough to forgive deception, to believe she hadn't intended to deceive?

They reached the pinnacle together, cried out together, and then became still and silent, together.

Val had to bolster her courage again. Rush was curled around her back, drowsy, his right arm draped over her waist. Val was tired but not drowsy. Her mind was going a mile a minute. She raised her head from the pillow and tried to see Rush over her shoulder.

"I have something to tell you," she said in a tremulous whisper.

"Don't tell me anything but that you love me."

"This is something you have to hear." Rush said nothing, but Val thought she detected a slight stiffening of his body. She let her head drop to the pillow and wriggled herself to her back. "Will you listen until I'm finished?"

Rush pushed up to an elbow. "No. I don't want to start any confessions from the past, not yours, not mine. Val, I trust you. Do you trust me?"

"Of course I trust you, but . . ."

He silenced her with a kiss that began tenderly and quickly evolved into desire. His lips became seductive then, and his tongue slid into her mouth to stroke and tease and tantalize.

He was breathing hard when he stopped kissing her, and his voice had become strained and husky. "We love each other, Val. That's all that matters now. I'll never question you again."

She touched his face in a pleading gesture. "Rush, this is something you should know."

"No, baby, no." He nipped at her lips. "I nearly destroyed what we have with my eternal prying." He tried to grin. "Do you know what I thought when I saw Tom's car? That he was your boyfriend."

Val's eyes widened. "Why on earth would you think that?"

"Because I saw him kiss you the day he came to the office. I didn't put it together with the man I'd been talking to on the phone until I saw his car this morning."

"He didn't . . ." Val's perplexed expression cleared. "Oh, yes, I forgot. He did kiss me, on the cheek. And you saw it?

That's why you began acting so cold? Oh, Rush, Tom and I hadn't seen each other in years, and that kiss meant nothing beyond . . ."

"I know, honey. I figured it out today. Look, that's all behind us, and that's where I intend to keep it. Will you indulge me?"

Val replied slowly. "If you're sure that's what you want. Be certain, though, please."

Rush smiled teasingly. "Did you kill anyone?"

Val managed a small laugh. "No."

"Are you secretly married?"

"Of course not."

"Then that's the end of it." Rush lowered his head for another kiss, and when he left her lips, his mouth traveled down her throat and to her breasts. He lingered at one lush nipple, then the other, and laughed deep in his throat because Val's response to his caresses was so evident.

But then, so was his own. He took Val's hand and brought it down his body. "See what you do to me, sweetheart? Let's not waste Tom's absence in idle chatter."

He'd spoken teasingly about "idle chatter," which Val fully recognized as a step toward making love again. Rush was certainly ready to do so, if what she was holding in her hand was any measure. He'd confessed his love and was past his previous serious stage, she realized, so maybe she shouldn't worry about his refusal to listen to her story.

She buried her concern and concentrated on the beautiful, sexy man in her arms, whom she loved with every portion of herself, imperfections and all. They made love slowly this time, with long, sensuous minutes of touching exploration and soft words of love.

Much later, when they were both utterly sated and barely with enough strength to speak, Val groggily checked the time. "It's getting late. I'd better go to my own bed before Tom gets home."

Rush moved languorously. "I suppose you should."

"We're both exhausted." Val pulled herself up and leaned over for a kiss. "Good night, my love. Sleep well."

Snuggled down in the master suite's king bed, Val yawned and stretched. Her body was warm and relaxed, and a most delicious sensation mellowed her thoughts. She was in love and was loved in return, a feeling like none other in her experience. Everything looked rosy; working with Rush would be exciting; being together after working hours would be...

She stiffened. Being together after working hours would be what? He still didn't know about her second career! He hadn't allowed her to speak, and come Tuesday night, or Wednesday night, clear through Saturday night, if he expected to see her, she would have to refuse. Why had she allowed him to detract her from her objective? Was she completely mindless? He *had* to know!

Tense again, Val threw back the covers and got up. She pulled on the caftan and hurried from the room to go to Rush's. But once there, standing by his bed, she didn't have the heart to wake him. Asleep, he looked sweet and young and guileless, and her hope for his understanding evolved into faith and trust that nothing could ever undo what had taken place here tonight. Alternatives to shaking him awake and startling him with a blurted, rather bizarre tale of a double life seemed feasible and sensible.

Silently Val stole away.

Val again occupied the back seat for the return trip to Las Vegas the next morning. She rode comfortably, with her head on the pillow, and sometimes her eyes were closed.

But she wasn't sleeping. Her lashes would lift to peer at Rush, and there were long stretches of just looking at him and reveling in the sight. She had categorized him as a playboy and careless at their first meeting, a hasty, unfair assessment based on his remarkable good looks and expensive clothes. She was guilty of bias without cause, and someday she would tell him about it.

But today, without fail, he would learn about "Valentine" and the Casbah. There were positive factors to relate, as well. Her dancing career was nearly over. The show's production manager had talked very fast in an attempt to convince her to stay, but even his offer of a sizable increase in pay hadn't tempted her. In two weeks, she would be plain Val LeClair in every segment of her life, and she could hardly wait.

Val only half listened to the front seat conversation, but it was evident that both Tom and Rush were excited about the Palm Springs project. She and Rush hadn't discussed it, but they would, she felt. Her opinion was positive, which she would be happy to tell him, though she would also emphasize that her opinion had little professional value and should not influence his decision.

But she suspected his decision was already made, which was fine with her. Anything Rush wanted to do was fine with her—anything at all. She smiled.

They pulled into the condo complex around noon. Rush walked her to her door and waited while she unlocked it. They went inside, where he immediately pulled her close for a kiss.

Aware that Tom hadn't driven away, Val snuggled closer and asked rather dreamily, "Aren't you staying?"

"Tom wants to walk through Saxon Springs. I'll spend a few hours with him and be back the minute I'm free." He kissed her again. "Don't pin up your hair, okay?"

Val smiled. "I won't."

"See you later." One more kiss, and Rush was gone. Wearing that dreamy, contented smile, Val closed the door behind him. She was happy, thrilled and already counting the time until Rush returned. Everything was going to be fine. Rush would probably laugh when she told him about her dual life, maybe praise her ingenuity. They were in love and nothing else mattered. She would present her story calmly and without guilt, and he would understand what had motivated her into drawing a line between her two careers.

After a few chores around the condo, Val took a shower and shampooed her hair. Slipping into a robe, she dried her mop of curls and fussed with it till it was perfect, and then did the same with cosmetics and her face. Checking the results in the mirror, Val surprised herself with a massive yawn. Five seconds later, she yawned again, and decided to catch a short nap before dressing for Rush's arrival.

She lay down carefully to avoid smearing her makeup, and fell asleep with a faint smile on her glossy lips.

Val awoke to a room gray with shadows, which took a few seconds to register. When the twilight sank in, she bolted upright and grabbed the clock from the bed stand. It was nearly eight. She had slept for hours.

"Damn," she muttered, leaping from the bed and awkwardly returning the clock to the bedstand. She raced through the condo to the front door and yanked it open, as though expecting Rush to be waiting on her stoop.

Feeling rather foolish, she closed the door and frowned. It was late in the day, and Rush had said he wouldn't be long. Wandering into the kitchen, Val spotted the blinking red light on her answering machine.

Amazed that she had slept through the ringing of the telephone, she pushed the Message button. Rush's voice clicked on.

"Sorry I missed you, honey. I'm flying to L.A. with Tom to meet a Kyle Peterson, whom Tom thinks is a possible third partner in the Palm Springs project. I'll tell you all about it when I get back, which should be sometime tomorrow afternoon. Keep the home fires burning, babe. I love you. See you tomorrow."

Val sat down, hard. Rush wasn't even in town, and this was her last night off before five consecutive nights of showtime at the Casbah. Disappointment wreaked havoc on Val's nervous system, disappointment and a renewal of dread.

This was not good. She had counted on tonight with Rush to get that explanation out of the way once and for all. He would want to see her tomorrow night, and explaining herself at the last minute wouldn't work nearly as well as a leisurely evening together.

The condo gradually darkened, and Val continued to sit and worry. Her only hope, she finally realized, was that Rush would call again this evening. A telephone connection was pretty cold fare in a situation like this, but it was better than no connection.

How in God's name had she slept through three rings of her telephone? Yes, she'd been burning the candle at both ends for a long time, but she must have passed out not to be roused by the phone.

Listlessly Val got up and switched on some lights.

Val was unusually busy at the Saxon Springs sales office the next morning. For some incalculable reason, swarms of looky-loos paraded through the models and then further frazzled her already frazzled nerves with dozens of questions. She passed out brochures and recited information until she felt numb, and then got a drink of water, took some deep breaths and began again.

Rush hadn't called again, not last night, not this morning. Val's nerves felt stretched to the breaking point. She feared the worst, which was Rush showing up just as she had to leave for the Casbah this evening.

She blamed only herself for this godawful situation. There'd been opportunities for frankness, and she should have insisted on Rush hearing her out. It was small comfort and no excuse for utter laxity in judgment that she swayed in whichever direction he indicated. Love made her as pliant as soft putty with Rush. He laid his hands on her and her will vanished. Obviously his was the more powerful personality, which, today, thinking about it, rubbed her the wrong way.

By four o'clock, Val was gritting her teeth. There was a couple in the office who seemed to have put down roots. They were possible buyers, but kept teetering back and forth on a decision.

Val sat at her desk, and the Haroldsons sat across from her. Val maintained a practiced smile while they argued.

"Honey," Bonnie Haroldson said in a whiny voice. "You said you liked the kitchen, now you're saying you don't?"

"I said it was adequate. Hell, I don't do the cooking. You decide on the kitchen and leave the garage to me."

"Well, isn't the garage all right?"

"I'm not sure it's big enough."

"What in heck would you do with a bigger one?"

When the phone rang, Val reached for it gratefully and murmured a polite "Excuse me" to the Haroldsons. "Saxon Springs," she said into the phone.

"Val? I'm glad I caught you."

Relief made Val weak. "Rush. Are you back in town?" The Haroldsons, she noticed, had stopped their irritating debate to listen.

"My flight gets in at nine-thirty tonight, honey."

"Nine-thirty!" Val was panicked. "Rush, I have to talk to you before then."

"I'll be home by ten, sweetheart. We can talk then."

Val swiveled her chair around and spoke as quietly as she could. "Rush, this is crucial. Can't you...?"

"What's crucial? Is there some kind of problem with the project?"

"No, no, it's nothing like that. Rush, I can't talk now. I have people at my desk. But it's imperative we talk as soon as possible."

"Well, that's going to be around ten tonight, Val. I'm at a pay phone, and Tom and Kyle are waiting in the car. I asked them to stop for just a minute when I spotted this phone. Look, whatever's going on, we'll discuss it thoroughly, I promise. Tom's deal looks good to me, Val, but I never did ask what you thought of it. That's why I'm calling. Your opinion is important to me. What do you think?"

"Oh, dear God," she moaned under her breath. "Tom's land looks perfect for development, but please don't base your decision on my opinion. Rush, listen...could you cal me at home before you get on the plane?"

"I can try. Val, this sounds serious."

"It is...and it isn't. But it is important. Call me, Rush. Promise."

"I'll do my best. Damn, you've got me worried now."

"No, don't be worried." Val could hear the Haroldsons fidgeting behind her. "Talk to you later, okay?"

"Right. Bye, honey."

Val put down the phone with a heavy sigh. Her smile across the desk was weary. "Sorry for the interruption. Let's get back to our discussion."

"Honey," Bonnie Haroldson said to her husband in her whiny voice. "I thought you liked the kitchen."

Twelve

Rush put in an exhilarating day in Southern California with Tom Delaney and Kyle Peterson. Where Tom approached business in an easygoing, rather humorous manner, Kyle was a dynamo of nervous energy, a small man who was rarely still, spoke rapidly and tossed ideas around until Rush's head spun.

One thing seemed certain: There was an education to be had in this world of wheeler-dealers. Business was vastly different than what Rush could have imagined. Ideas blossomed from other ideas. Meeting one person led to an introduction to someone else, and then to someone else again. Everyone had his or her own irons in the fire, and was willing, even eager, to talk about them. There seemed to be a circuit of investors and entrepreneurs, men and women with big ideas and the ambition and know-how to make them work, and Rush met quite a number of them at Kyle's insistence.

Not only that, he hauled Tom and Rush all over Southern California, driving and talking and waving his arms, all at the same time, showing them numerous pieces of vacant land and projects already underway, properties in which he owned an interest. He talked trades, and partnerships, and joint ventures, and mentioned six-and seven-digit figures as though speaking of pennies.

Rush was impressed. Not completely sold on everything he saw and everyone he met, but impressed nonetheless. This was a world he hadn't known existed, and it stirred his imagination and raised his blood pressure. His grandfather had been a part of it, he realized at some point of the energizing day, and what a pity the old gentleman hadn't included his grandsons.

It was during a harried run with Tom through the airport to catch their return flight to Vegas that Rush remembered his promise to call Val again. His stomach sank clear to his toes, and settling himself in his seat on the plane, he lost his newly gained enthusiasm for business and worried about what he'd overlooked during the day's bustle.

Not calling again was unforgivable. If Val was angry when he saw her, he had no defense. Getting caught up in Kyle's whirlwind tour was no excuse for such a blatant lack of consideration. This was no way to begin a permanent relationship, especially when he was madly in love with the lady.

Tom was sitting in the adjoining seat with his head back. "Tom? Could I ask you a personal question?"

Tom turned his gaze to Rush. "Go ahead."

"How do you manage to do so much traveling?" Rush frowned. "What I mean is, you obviously have a strong marriage, and how does a man juggle business pressures and good intentions?"

Tom grinned. "Thinking of tying the knot with someone?"

"That someone is Val."

A light came on in Tom's gray eyes. "Congratulations."

"Congratulations might be a bit premature. I promised to call her before the flight and didn't do it."

"Oh, oh," Tom said sympathetically. "Women are funny about things like that. A man should never make a promise he can't keep."

"I really meant to do it," Rush said grimly. "Would your wife be upset if she expected a call that never came?"

"You'd better believe it. Pam and I've done our adjusting, make no mistake. You and Val will, too. It takes time." Tom smiled consolingly. "Once the kinks are worked out of a marriage, it's the best of all relationships, Rush."

"I'm sure you're right. What bothers me is Val mentioning a problem when I talked to her earlier," Rush confided. "She said it was crucial that we spoke again before I got on the plane."

"Didn't she give you a hint as to the nature of the problem?"

"She couldn't speak freely. There were people at her desk."

They fell silent, as though the subject was too complicated for simple discussion. When the plane reached altitude and the Fasten Seat Belt sign was turned off, they put their seats back and closed their eyes.

Rush felt wired. The prolonged, avid excitement from the day and his tension over that missed phone call was an unnerving combination of emotions. He willed the flight to be over quickly, and visualized himself facing Val with enough guilt to warrant a prison sentence.

This love thing had a million subtleties, he thought uneasily. And a lot of unwritten, unstated rules. He'd learned one of them today: Don't promise to call and then not follow through.

Rush sighed to himself. Every couple in serious love must go through the same trial and error period. Tom had admitted he and Pam had, and apparently they were a couple with a solid relationship. That's what Rush wanted with Val, but after his faux pas today, she might have other ideas.

There would be no more side trips tonight, Rush ardently vowed. If Tom couldn't drive him directly home from the airport for some reason, he would take a taxi. Val would be waiting for him, of that he was positive.

The flight *was* short. Not because Rush had willed it, but because the distance between Los Angeles and Las Vegas was merely a hop for a jet plane. They deplaned as hastily as traffic allowed, with Rush barely able to conceal his impatience.

In the concourse, Rush dashed to the nearest phone, inserted a quarter and dialed Val's number. When he got her answering machine, he held the phone out and looked at it disbelievingly. Hanging up, he repeated the process with a second quarter.

Tom was idling a few feet away. Rush slammed the phone on the hook. "She isn't home!"

With an innocent expression, Tom looked the other way. Rush started walking, staying three steps ahead of Tom all the way through the airport to the parking garage.

They got into the BMW, with Rush grim and Tom silent. Finally, nearly halfway to Rush's and Val's condo complex, Rush stated angrily, "I don't get it. She said it was important to talk to me, and she's not home."

Tom cleared his throat and kept on driving. Rush peered at him. "Don't you think that's peculiar?"

"Hey, Rush, don't put me in between you and Val. You're both good friends of mine."

Rush let out a heavy sigh and tried to calm himself. "Sorry, Tom." But after a minute he repeated, "I just don't get it."

The BMW drove through the front gate of the complex. Rush stated with forced calm, "I'll get out at my place and put my bag inside before going to Val's."

"Sure, Rush."

Parked in front of Rush's condo, he turned in the seat and offered his hand. "Thanks for everything, Tom. I appreciate the trip and meeting Kyle."

They shook hands. "I'll be in McCall for the rest of this week, Rush. Think about the Palm Springs project. I feel pretty certain Kyle will get involved. If everyone's in agreement, the three of us should get together again when I get back."

"Sounds good to me, Tom. Thanks again."

While Tom drove away, Rush sprinted up the sidewalk to his front door, unlocked it, opened it enough to slide his overnight bag inside and closed it again. In three minutes flat, he was ringing Val's doorbell.

A light was on inside, but Val didn't answer. Rush stood on her stoop and tried to make sense of her absence. Was she so furious he hadn't called that she was deliberately somewhere else?

Or was she where she usually went at night, wherever in hell *that* was!

Furious himself, Rush trudged back to his own place. But going to bed as though everything was peachy was out of the question. He paced and cussed and kicked the hassock in Larry's living room. And after an hour of trying Val's phone number every ten minutes, he grabbed his car keys and stormed out to the garage.

Gunning the MG's engine, he drove out of the complex and onto the street. He'd thought Val's nightly disappearances were a thing of the past. Where did she go? What did she do?

He drove aimlessly, but gradually gravitated toward the Strip. The warm night air ruffled his hair. He stopped at red lights and shifted gears automatically, his expression grim, his thoughts muddled and on Val. Spotting a pay phone outside a convenience store, he pulled into the parking lot and got out to try Val's number again. Her voice on the answering machine refueled his anger, and he drove off muttering.

Reaching the Strip altered his mood slightly. The traffic was bumper to bumper. Crowds of people trod the sidewalks and crosswalks. Brightly colored neon bulbs blazed from hundreds of massive signs, turning night into a garish facsimile of day. He drove the entire Strip, made a U-turn when the street headed into the downtown area and drove it again, finding an oblique sort of comfort in the crowds, the lights, the noise and activity.

On impulse he turned into the entrance of a large hotel-casino, the Casbah. Leaving the MG with a valet parking attendant, he strode through the nearest of the resort's several front doors.

The casino was alive and throbbing with music, laughter, voices and the smell and sound of money. Coins rattled in and out of machines, bells rang, lights flashed. Rush joined the melee without purpose, and slowly wandered past the dozens of blackjack tables, then the dice tables. He had no desire to gamble himself, but watching those who did took his mind off Val.

He noticed a line of people outside the resort's showroom, and another impulse had him buying a ticket and joining the queue. Inside the showroom, after a brief wait, he was shown to a long table already crowded with people and drinks. He sat down.

The man on his left turned and grinned. "All by yourself, pal?"

"Yes." Rush scanned the table. Everyone there was part of a group; he was the only sore thumb.

He ordered Perrier water instead of alcohol, preferring to get home in one piece. Two glasses were placed in front of him, as two drinks of choice were included in the price of the ticket. Conversation at the table ebbed and flowed, interspersed with bursts of excited laughter. The hum and buzz of hundreds of people in the showroom created a din increased in volume by the orchestra warming up.

The lights went down. Thundering applause broke out as the elaborate curtains opened to a dark stage. A laser beam of light suddenly knifed the blackness, then another, and another, until the stage area looked like a distorted, wildly colored checkerboard of moving lights and patterns. The music swelled, and suddenly, from out of nowhere it seemed, the huge stage was teeming with activity, men and women in motion.

Their costumes were spectacular, the light and color almost blinding, the music filling every corner of the large showroom. Rush was mesmerized in spite of his foul mood. There were singers, and dancers, and so much to see, he couldn't take it all in. The women were beautiful, the men handsome, and there was enough talent on that big stage to cast a hundred Hollywood films.

A voice boomed through the sound system. "Ladies and gentlemen. The Casbah is proud to present... *Valentine!*"

A woman appeared in center stage and began to dance with two young men. Her costume was sparkling blue, the men's were red, and all of them covered only the essentials. Their dancing was fluid, energetic, technically complicated and beautiful to watch. The woman was passed back and forth between the men. She spun, she leapt, she gyrated.

Valentine. Rush squinted his eyes to see her better. It hadn't occurred to him when seated that his assigned table was a long way from the stage. The woman's hair touched a familiar chord, and so did her figure and legs. Yet the idea was so preposterous, all he could do was sweat over it.

But the longer he watched, the more panicked he felt. He overheard whispered comments between two men. "Damn, would you look at the hooters on that babe?" "I sure wouldn't kick her out of my bed."

Rush kept getting stiffer, and more dry-mouthed. He drained his two glasses of sparkling water while staring at the stage and Valentine.

Valentine. Val. It couldn't be. It wasn't possible.

He stumbled to his feet and to the main door, where he located the maître d'. "I need to get closer to the stage," he mumbled, holding out a twenty-dollar bill.

The suave man in a tuxedo smoothly palmed the bill. "Follow me, sir. Watch your step."

Rush was delivered to a prime table. He sat down slowly, his eyes never leaving the stage. The music had become a too-loud roar in his ears. For him the crowd and everyone else on stage vanished. All he saw was Val—*Valentine*—bending, swaying, moving. This close, he could see her stage makeup, and the slight sheen of perspiration on her skin. She was beautiful, sensuous, one second a sprite, the next a siren.

This was where she spent her nights. The shock was too much to assimilate. Rush sat as though frozen. He felt betrayed, degraded, yet had no ability to isolate and identify the debilitating sensations.

When he could take no more, he reached into his pocket for a pen and scribbled on a cocktail napkin. *Val, I'm in the audience. Meet me in the lounge outside the showroom. Rush.* He staggered to his feet, found a waiter and held out another twenty. "Would you see that Val LeClair...I mean, Valentine, gets this."

"I'll have it delivered backstage, sir."

Somehow Rush made it out of the showroom without tripping over something. The casino seemed quiet by comparison. He stood beyond the doors, dazed, and sucked in air, as though he'd been deprived of oxygen for the last twenty or so minutes.

On unsteady legs, he trekked to the lounge and fell into a booth. Almost immediately a scantily clad cocktail waitress appeared. "What can I get you, sir?"

"A double scotch, neat. And a tall glass of water," he called as the woman walked away.

The drinks arrived before Rush had recovered. He stared at the scotch and wondered if he would *ever* recover, then reached for the glass of water. He couldn't start drinking booze, he thought bitterly. He might never stop.

The glass of scotch was left untouched, but Rush drank three glasses of water while he waited for the show to be over. He kept asking himself why. Why hadn't Val told him? Why was she doing this? Why had she lied...and betrayed...and deceived? Why had she told him she loved him? Why had she let him fall in love with her?

The water sloshed in his stomach and demanded a trip to the men's room. He ran there and back, afraid he might miss Val.

The showroom emptied. Hordes of people passed by the lounge. He watched for Val, searching the crowd, straining to see her in the mass.

An hour later he realized she wasn't coming. The showroom was dark, the lounge was vacant...even the casino was thinly occupied. Dull-minded from exhaustion and a ponderous sorrow, Rush got up and headed across the casino to the front door.

He had no idea what he might do next.

Val went into her condo and immediately checked the answering machine. Its red light blinked repeatedly. Quickly she pushed the Message button, and her mouth got tighter with each indication of another hang-up. It had to be Rush. No one else she knew called again and again without saying something.

She was tense about him not calling earlier. Apparently he'd waited until he got back to Vegas, and he was probably furious she hadn't answered. Val's mouth got tighter still. Other than fantastic sex, their relationship was little more than a disturbing series of misunderstandings, and she was becoming weary of the game.

It was late, but his last call hadn't been that long ago. Val picked up the phone and dialed Larry's condo. She waited through seven rings, then hung up with a frown. Rush wasn't home. How...peculiar.

Her routine had not gone well tonight. She had danced clumsily, missing time and steps. Her mind had not been in sync with her body, and it took concentration to perform with precision. But even now, she felt emotionally disconnected from her exhausted arms and legs. Working two jobs for so long was finally catching up with her. She had suspected it would happen, but it wasn't possible to ignore Rush's role in her fatigue. Pressure was never pleasant, and maybe she'd caused most of it herself, but shouldn't falling in love free one's spirit rather than making a person feel smothered?

Val put the teakettle on the stove and then changed her mind in the next instant. Snapping off lights, she dragged herself to her bedroom, undressed and crawled into bed naked, too tired to worry about a nightgown. Her last thought before dropping into a deep sleep was about Rush: If he was angry because she wasn't home when he finally got around to calling, he could take a flying leap at the moon. She'd tried to explain herself in Palm Springs, and he hadn't let her.

Driving past Val's condo, Rush saw the dark windows, which had been lighted earlier. He stopped the MG at the curb and broodingly stared at the silent scene. Very few of the other condos had lights on. It was late, nearly three.

But Val was home now. Anger churned in Rush's gut, mingling with his wounded pride and sense of betrayal. Why should she sleep when he knew damned well he wouldn't? She owed him an explanation, though his need to hear it warred with dread. Regardless, something was driving him. He not only wouldn't sleep, but he wouldn't get anything else done until he confronted Val. She would be at the sales office in the morning, but it was too public for the feelings broiling in his blood.

He turned off the ignition and got out. His walk to Val's front door was stiff and graceless. His body ached as well as his soul, and he leaned on the bell with his jaw clenched.

There was no sound from inside, and he swore he'd ring that bell until it wore out before giving up. He could hear the repeating chimes, over and over, the same two tones. *Ding-dong, ding-dong*. How could she sleep through it?

Val couldn't wake up. Something was dinging, incessantly. Her eyes opened a hairbreadth. The room was dark. What was that sound?

The doorbell. A groan welled in Val's throat. "Go away." She pulled the pillow over her head. The bell didn't stop. With her eyes barely open, she crawled out of bed and dragged on a robe. Her trip to the front door was in slow motion. Yawning, she looped the sash of the robe around her waist.

"Who's there?"

Rush's eyes narrowed. "It's Rush."

Val sagged against the wall next to the door. She couldn't think, and was barely managing to stay upright. "Rush..." she mumbled.

"Open the door, Val."

"Go away, Rush." She started to shuffle back to bed.

"Val!"

He was yelling her name. She turned to the door. "Stop yelling! You'll wake the entire complex. I'll be at the office in the morning."

"I need to talk to you tonight! Open the damned door or I swear I'll kick it in!"

"You'll what?" Val slid back the dead bolt. The door burst open and Rush came in. "What's wrong with you?" She still couldn't think. Her brain was fuzzy, and her eyes wouldn't focus. She squinted at him. "What time is it?"

"Ten to three."

"I just got to bed an hour ago," she said disgustedly, and then yawned. "I'm dead on my feet. Be nice and go away, okay?"

Rush's back was to the door. His glaring scrutiny took in her tumbled hair and her robe that was only partially closed, leaving an inch-wide gap that exposed bare skin. His jaw tensed. "I'm not going away. We're going to talk."

Val's mouth stretched with an enormous yawn. "*You* might be going to talk. I'm going back to bed." She started away. "Close the door when you leave. I don't give a damn if it's locked or not."

"Val! Or maybe you prefer *Valentine*."

She turned, slowly. "What did you say?"

"That got your attention, didn't it? How in hell long did you plan to play me for a fool?"

Her brain began whirling with a feverish dread. She gave her head a sharp, clearing shake and touched her fingertips to her forehead. He knew, and she hadn't told him. But someone had. This was all wrong. This conversation should not be taking place at three in the morning with her exhausted and him angry.

Val was coming awake fast. Her narrowed eyes focused on the fury and resentment in Rush's expression. He was angry. Why? Yes, he should have learned the truth from her rather than from someone else, but there were hordes of mitigating circumstances and his anger wasn't fair.

She took a breath, willing away the sudden churning anxiety in her stomach. "I never played you for a fool, Rush. Don't accuse me of something I'm not even capable of doing."

His angry smirk cut her to the quick. "I doubt if there's very much you're *not* capable of doing. You put on an act from the moment we met. You deliberately led me to believe you were an unpretentious, guileless woman intent on a real estate career. Instead you're a . . ."

Val held up a frantic hand. "Stop! You're judging me without hearing my side. Rush, I tried to talk about this in Palm Springs. Be honest with both of us. Didn't I make several attempts to tell you something? Didn't you refuse to listen? Didn't you talk about trusting being all that mattered?"

Rush's eyes were dark and glittering. "I marvel that you dare even mention the word *trust*. And don't throw back at me anything I said in Palm Springs. I thought I knew you then, and all I knew was the phony woman you presented to me. Besides, why should I believe you were trying to tell me about your other life? Why should I believe anything you might say now?''

He'd pronounced *other life* as though she was guilty of the lowest form of human depravity. Val's legs nearly gave out. Tears were very close, gathering behind her eyes and stinging her nose. In all of her life she had never felt such soul-shattering pain as what weakened her now.

"I . . . have to sit down," she whispered, and moved into the living room to sink onto a chair. She felt a flash of gratitude because Rush followed; if he had chosen to leave instead, she would not have had the strength to stop him, and they had to talk. *Dear God, this couldn't end yet.*

Yet she didn't know what to say. He was standing in the middle of her living room and looking at her with hard eyes, and the whole awful mess only went round and round in her mind in such a tight ball of miserable facts and fancy, she could find no loose end with which to start.

One idea worked to the surface. "Who told you?" she asked raggedly.

"No one told me. I had the good fortune to find it out for myself."

He'd spoken sarcastically, cynically, with hurt pride and shattered ego underlying every syllable. Val shuddered. "How?"

"I went to the Casbah tonight. I was in the audience." Rush's gaze turned as cold as ice. "Why did you leave me hanging in the lounge?"

"In the lounge?" Val echoed hoarsely. He'd been in the audience? He'd walked into that showroom unaware and seen her on stage, just like that? Her insides seemed to compress into a solid block of empathetic agony. No one should have to face the kind of shock Rush must have received in that audience, no one. "Why . . . did you think I would be in the lounge?" she whispered.

"Because of the note I sent backstage," Rush snarled.

"Oh, God." Val groaned. "Rush, I get notes almost every night. I never read them."

"That's just great." Rush circled the room, every line of his body conveying tension, anger, frustration. "I waited for hours."

"I'm sorry. Rush, I'm so sorry."

He swung around. "I'll just bet you are."

Val realized then that he was not going to accept any apology she might make. His anger had reached the unreasonable stage. Maybe his pride had been dealt such an astronomical blow he would never forgive her.

But her own pride wasn't in the best of shape right now, either. "I tried to tell you," she said in a stronger voice that also turned some of the blame for tonight's fiasco on him. "You wouldn't listen."

"Your attempted confession was a trifle belated, don't you think?" Rush sneered.

"Confession!" Val teetered to her feet. "Don't interpret my explanation as a confession, Rush. I'm not the least bit ashamed of my *other life,* as you put it, nor was I looking for your approval when I tried to explain myself."

"I don't believe you were ever going to tell me."

"That's absurd!" Val cried. "How could we have a future together if you didn't know? Why do you think I asked you to call me before you got on the plane? I had to go back to work tonight, and I knew—*thought*—you'd want to see me when you got back from L.A. Rush, don't twist this into some sort of... of impossible plot to delude you. The truth is complex enough without exaggerating it further. I never meant to..."

"Were you thinking of a future together, Val? Were you thinking at all? Can you even imagine how I felt seeing you on that stage without the slightest warning?"

Val was still having some trouble with the concept of such an unlikely coincidence. "Tom never... hinted?"

Rush's face got darker. "Tom knew? Did everyone in the whole damned state know but me?" His fury suddenly went wild, and he knew he had to get out of there. Whirling, he started for the door.

"Wait!" From behind him Val frantically grabbed his arm. "Rush, you're not being fair! Aren't you going to let me explain?"

He threw off her hand. "I got an explanation earlier tonight, *Valentine*," he snarled. "And it'll do me for the rest of my life, lady."

His words felt like a slap in the face. Val drew herself up. "That's it then?"

"For us? What do you think?"

She hadn't completely absorbed his meaning yet; that would come later. Her anger had been slow in developing, but his righteous attitude, his censure and his refusal to discuss this rationally had finally driven hope from her system. Anger was her only defense against such an enormous loss.

"In that case," she said coldly, "consider our business arrangement terminated."

Taken aback, Rush looked at her queerly. "You don't intend to sell the remaining homes in the project?"

"I think not."

His temper erupted again. "That suits me just fine!"

Val didn't move for the longest time. Her front door slammed shut. The MG started and drove away, and still she stood there.

It's over, she thought dully. Really over. Had her sin been terrible enough for this conclusion? Was protecting one's privacy a sin at all? Who was Rush Saxon to judge anyone so harshly? Wasn't he deliberately allowing Tom to believe he possessed more experience in business than was true? Was her omission of personal information any worse than his?

Val started for the telephone to tell him to clean up his own act before judging her so cold-bloodedly, then changed her mind. Wearily she trudged off to bed.

Thirteen

This was a period of transition for Val. Instead of holding down two full-time jobs, she found herself facing none. Locating a broker with whom to hang her real estate license would not be a difficult undertaking, but it wasn't a decision she wanted to make overnight. As in every field, there were considerations—commission percentages, advertising exposure and reputation, to name a few that any ambitious Realtor should weigh when choosing a broker.

At least that was the argument Val kept presenting herself with when days passed and she didn't go out looking for that broker. In truth, she couldn't muster any interest or ambition. For the first time in her adult life she drifted, with sleeping as much as possible, tending to the condo and going to the Casbah becoming her daily routine.

Rush was on her mind constantly. She understood his anger and couldn't resent him for breaking their ties. At times she mentally built a good case for what she'd done. Logic and basic human rights were on her side. Privacy was a valuable commodity, and she was as entitled to her opinions and outlook as Rush was to his.

But logic had very little influence with emotion. Val's hurting went soul deep and felt like a permanent fixture. Immediately after their confrontation, it occurred to her that Rush might be angry enough to notify the title companies to withhold payment of her commissions. If that should happen, her only recourse would be to sue him, a prospect that gave her cold chills.

She was relieved enough to get weak knees when a commission check arrived in the mail, her first from the Saxon Springs project. In a few days, another check came, and then a third. Apparently Rush hadn't interfered with that aspect of their business arrangement, which gave Val a modicum of hope that his anger might abate.

But she never saw him beyond spotting his car once in a while. She drove past the project and the company office, and occasionally caught a glimpse of the MG going in or out of the condo complex, but that was the extent of it.

In the meantime, her last night of performing on stage arrived without fanfare. Some of the cast members brought a cake backstage and held a small so-long-and-good-luck party after the show; but as Val had requested no publicity from the production manager, there wasn't even a small article in the paper about Valentine's retirement.

Instead, she noticed in the next morning's paper that a large ad had been inserted announcing the Casbah's new star: *Margot!* Val smiled and looked inwardly for nostalgia, or any traces of regret. There were none. She had reached her goal and it felt wonderful.

But it was the only wonderful thing in her life at the present, if one discounted the satisfaction she felt every time she received a commission check and wrote one of her own to chip away at those medical bills. For years she had made nominal payments, and to write a check for a thousand dollars, or two thousand, was indeed satisfying. In calculating her total commissions earned on the Saxon project, she would be able to wipe out those old debts and still have a little money in the bank for herself.

A few days after her final performance at the Casbah, Val was outside watering the clay pot of marigolds on her front stoop. With September the weather had made a delightful turn, dropping a good twenty-five degrees on the thermometer. This was the time of year Val liked best. Falls were glorious in Southern Nevada, and winters, for the most part, never got beyond comfortably cool. There were months and months of great weather to look forward to, and Val didn't think about next July and August if she could help it.

She set the watering can down and bent over to pinch off some drying blossoms, when she heard a car stopping at the curb. Looking up, she smiled and straightened. It was Tom's BMW.

"Hello, Val," Tom called as he came up the walk.

"Hi, Tom. How are you?"

"Couldn't be better. How're you doing?"

Val wondered how much, if anything, Tom knew about her and Rush's break. "I'm fine, Tom. Come inside," Val invited. "I just made a pitcher of lemonade."

"Thanks. I can't stay long, but I'd like a glass of lemonade," Tom said as they filed through the front door. "Pam and I are having guests for dinner and I told her I'd get home early."

Val saw Tom to the living room and then went to the kitchen. She returned in a minute with two tall glasses, one of which she passed to Tom before seating herself on the sofa. "Pam is back from McCall now?"

"Yes, and she wants to meet you. When would be a good time for the three of us to get together? I know your working schedule is hectic, what with your job at the Casbah, so we're leaving it up to you."

Val placed her glass on a coaster. "I don't work at the Casbah anymore, Tom."

"You really did quit?" Tom questioned with some surprise.

"That's been my plan for a year now," Val told him.

"Yes, you mentioned that. So it's going to be just real estate from now on."

Val smiled. "As soon as I line up a broker, yes."

"Rush said Saxon Springs is completely sold-out. You did a bang-up job with that project, Val."

"Well...someone else made the last few sales, Tom. I haven't been involved for several weeks now."

Tom frowned. "Funny. Rush never said anything about that. We've been seeing quite a lot of each other, too. The Palm Springs project is a go, and it's taking up a great deal of our time. But he never mentions—" Tom's frown deepened "—you." He immediately looked chagrined. "I'm sorry, Val. I didn't mean to stick my nose into your private life. In Rush's, either."

"It's all right, Tom. Rush and I had a...falling out." Val forced a smile. "I'm glad the project is sold-out for his sake, whoever handled the final sales."

"I'll let you in on something, Val," Tom said slowly. "I've been thinking of asking you to get your California license and come to work on the Palm Springs project."

"Tom, I doubt if Rush would agree. Apparently you haven't discussed that idea with him. And maybe you shouldn't," Val added after a pause. Apparently Rush didn't mention her at all, which was both comforting and disturbing. At least he wasn't bad-mouthing her, but had he actually succeeded in putting her so completely out of his mind that he didn't slip and say her name by accident?

Val felt terribly defeated, though she tried hard to conceal it from her guest's eyes. "Would you like some more lemonade?" she asked brightly.

"No, thanks. I only stopped for a minute to let you know Pam was back. Think about when we might get together and let me know, all right?"

"Yes, I will," Val promised while walking Tom to the door.

She stood on her front stoop and watched the BMW drive away, then picked up the watering can and tried to see the marigolds through the mist of tears in her eyes.

Rush spotted the BMW driving up through the front windows of the company office. As he hadn't expected Tom to come by today, the visit surprised him.

He went outside to greet him. "Hi. Just in the neighborhood?"

"More or less," Tom replied.

"Come on in," Rush invited. Inside he offered, "Coffee? Water? A soft drink?"

"Nothing, thanks. I just had some lemonade at Val's place. Rush, I didn't know you two were on the outs. You never said anything."

"No, I didn't," Rush quietly concurred. "It wasn't something I wanted to talk about."

Tom chose a chair and sat down. "Well, I'm not trying to pry or interfere in any way. But I've been thinking about Val working on the Palm Springs project for some time now, and I need to hear how you might feel about that idea. She did a hell of a job here. It takes Val's kind of dedication to get a project moving, but if her presence would bother you..."

Rush frowned. "I doubt if she'd be interested, Tom. Don't forget she quit this project because of..." He raked his hair. "Hell, I might as well say it like it is. She quit because of me." His gaze settled on his friend's face. "You knew about her job at the Casbah." Tom nodded. "Do you know why she kept it a secret from me?"

Tom cleared his throat. "Rush, one thing I learned a long time ago was to stay out of people's personal lives. Especially people I'm doing business with. Why don't you ask Val?"

Rush had thought of that question a hundred times himself. But he'd been trying desperately to forget Val, deliberately recalling that night whenever his anger lost impetus.

She had caused one of the worst blows of his life, unnecessarily. He couldn't imagine a sensible reason for keeping that side of herself from him, and when he remembered how she had disguised her looks with an ugly hairstyle and humdrum clothing, he saw red again. He had loved her, and she had betrayed him. It was that simple.

But that didn't mean he would deter her involvement with the Palm Springs project. "Look," he said to Tom. "If you think Val is the right salesperson for Palm Springs, I won't stand in the way."

"It's your decision as much as mine," Tom reminded.

"And Kyle's," Rush said pointedly.

Tom got to his feet. "Tell you what. Let's discuss it at next week's partnership meeting. That'll give all of us a little time to consider our options."

Rush stood up. "Did you say anything to Val about it yet?"

"Only in passing, Rush. No promises were made by either Val or myself."

Uneasily Rush followed his friend to the door. At the last second he finalized a decision that had been brewing since the night he and Val had had it out. "Tom, there's another matter we need to discuss."

"What's that?" Tom asked.

"I haven't been completely up-front with you."

Tom raised an eyebrow. "In what way?"

"It's about my background," Rush said firmly. "Saxon Springs is my first practical experience with business. I've let you believe otherwise. I guess I wouldn't blame you if you asked for my resignation from the California partnership."

Tom became thoughtful. "From what I've seen at Saxon Springs, you're no slouch in business, Rush. Maybe you didn't know, but the project's sorry state before you took over was pretty common knowledge." He offered his hand. "But I appreciate the honesty. Thanks."

After Tom had gone, Rush sat at his desk again feeling a if he'd just lost a hundred-pound burden. He had never ou and out lied to Tom about his business experience, but let ting Tom live with an erroneous opinion had been almost a deceitful as Val had been with him.

"Almost" was a word with enormous subtleties, how ever. Every time he thought of Val's deception, the pain re turned all over again. And yet, the day would come when h would have to face her again. Tom and Kyle held great hope for the Palm Springs property, and if Val was the best sales person for the job, then she should do it. Personal prob lems had no place in a business deal. Tom lived by tha credo, and Rush couldn't fault the practice.

Rush slapped his palms on the desk and stood up. Run ning into Val eventually was inevitable, and he might as wel get their initial meeting over with. Besides, there was some thing else she should hear from him: She was going to re ceive commissions on the last sales in the Saxon Spring project.

Rush didn't see his largesse as charity. Without Val, tha project would have stood every chance of going straigh down the drain and they both knew it.

It was, at the very least, a sound reason for paying her visit.

Val was washing salad vegetables at the kitchen sink whe she glanced out the window and saw Rush's MG pulling u at the curb. Her heart nearly stopped and then starte pounding. Clumsily she turned off the faucet and dried he hands.

How did she look? Her still damp hands darted to he hair. She was wearing a sundress, nothing fancy though sh hadn't worried about it when Tom stopped by, and th makeup she'd put on earlier in the day had to be all bu gone.

She could look a hundred times better than she did, she decided unhappily, but there was no time for repairs: Rush was ringing her bell.

Val took a minute, hoping to calm her racing pulse. He could be here for a dozen reasons, she frantically told herself. He wasn't necessarily at her door because of her. Maybe there was a snag in some of the closings. Maybe he needed her intervention with some of the buyers.

She didn't run to the foyer, though every impulse urged her to do so. When she opened the door, she looked quite calm, a supreme effort.

"Hello, Rush." Her eyes met his and she found his expression to be unreadable.

"Hello, Val. Mind if I come in for a minute?"

"Not at all." Holding the door, she stepped back. With that blank look in his eyes, she was positive he was here on business. It was a calamitous feeling to be this close to him and know she meant nothing to him. Painful and sad and tragic, because the whole thing had happened without malice.

"Come into the living room," she said evenly, marveling that her voice didn't crack.

"Thanks."

They paraded silently into the living room and sat down. "Could I get you something to drink?" Val asked in a polite tone of voice.

"Nothing, thanks." Rush wasn't comfortable, and he leaned forward with his forearms on his knees. "I guess you saw Tom today."

"He stopped in for a few minutes, yes."

Rush looked down at his hands. This was a lot tougher than he'd supposed. "I . . ." His eyes lifted. She looked so beautiful, and it wasn't possible to be with her and not remember. His feelings for her had been important, serious, and certainly his physical awareness of her hadn't been destroyed by anger. He should have realized this would happen. He should have known that being in the same room with her would make him ache and yearn and wish to God he'd never gone to the Casbah that night.

"What is it, Rush?" Why was he here? His expression was peculiar, uncertain, unnerving Val.

Sitting back in a deliberate attempt to appear non-plussed, he managed a weak smile. "I'd like to clear the air. Tom mentioned the possibility of your handling the sales for the Palm Springs project. It's okay with me."

"How generous of you," Val said with cool observation. "But since the subject seems to have come up only today, I think it's an idea everyone needs to give some thought to before making any decisions."

"Well, yes, I agree. But I wanted you to know how I felt about it."

A silence stretched until Val asked, "Was there anything else?"

"Yes. I really came by to tell you that you'll be receiving your normal commissions on the project's final sales."

Val raised a surprised eyebrow. "Why?"

"If you want a logical answer, it's because the buyers were comebacks. But even if they hadn't been, I'd feel obligated to honor our contract." He hesitated a moment, then said quietly, "I'm sorry you felt it necessary to cancel our business arrangement."

Val batted her lashes to hold back the sudden spate of tears stinging her eyes. "You left me very little choice that night. You're a . . . hard man, Rush," she whispered.

"Me?" he said in genuine astonishment. "That's not true, Val."

"You judged me from the moment we met, and harshly."

The accusation hit home, startling Rush. His own memory proved it accurate. But he'd never meant to judge, and certainly not harshly. He'd just seen so much potential for beauty in Val, and had rued her disregard of it.

His defenses arose. His attitude, overbearing or not, didn't excuse Val's deception. She had deliberately shut him out of a major portion of her life, and he would never forget the pain of that night in the Casbah's showroom.

He slid to the edge of the sofa cushion and got to his feet. "Let's not start accusing each other, Val. It would only lead to more dissension, which I'm sure you don't need any more than I do."

With sudden panic she watched him getting up. He was going to leave, and if she let him walk out that door, they would never see each other again, not in the way she wanted.

Rush saw her rising. "You don't need to get up. I can see myself out."

"I'm not in the mood for good manners and a polite goodbye," Val said flatly. Her teary sensation had vanished, replaced by an almost icy pragmatism. "There are a few things that need saying, and I would appreciate your listening to me."

He'd never heard Val speak in that exact tone before. Her voice wasn't emotional. Rather, it had a steely edge, and seemingly immovable strength.

"I didn't come here to fight with you, Val."

"No, you came here to get rid of a problem with money." Val needed those additional commissions, but she'd be damned if she'd trade her self-respect for a few extra dollars. "Maybe money has solved your problems in the past, Rush, but I think you owe me something more than cash."

"I owe you?" Rush said with a twist of his lips that struck Val as just a bit smug. "I didn't assign you those commissions because of any sense of debt, Val, nor to ease my conscience. What've I got to feel guilty about, anger? Resentment? Think again, Val. Your little charade caused the whole damned thing. Don't worry. I'll never step foot in the Casbah again."

"It's immaterial to me whether you do or don't. I don't work there anymore."

The news struck Rush right between the eyes. "Why not?"

"Are you truly interested in my answer, or was that question merely caused by surprise?"

"Uh . . . surprise, I guess," he admitted. At the instantly angry expression on her face, he added, "Well, what the hell do you expect me to say? Why wouldn't I be surprised? Obviously that career meant more to you than anything else in your life!"

"That arrogant remark *proves* how little you know about it!" Val shrieked. Instantly she calmed herself. "Did you or did you not tell me you loved me?" she asked.

Rush hadn't expected her to go for the jugular, and he suddenly wasn't quite so sure of himself. "I said it," he admitted darkly. "And so did you. So much for bedroom confessions."

Val covered her wince. "Maybe it was only a bedroom confession to you, but I happen to be in love with you."

He blanched. He stood there and stared at her and turned ashen. "Val . . ."

She was glad to have shaken him. He needed a good shaking more than any person she'd ever known. Before he walked out of her front door, he was going to hear it all.

"Let's clear up a few historical facts, okay? I decided to get out of show business shortly after my mother died," she said coolly. "Thirty isn't old in most professions, but nearly all of the other dancers in the show are ten years younger. I was as eager as they are when I started out. I made a good salary, and I loved the excitement of performing onstage.

"But attitude and what constitutes excitement for a person changes with time. Working five nights a week became monotonous, tiresome and eventually unbearable. There were aspects of the business I learned to loathe, men sending nasty little notes backstage, for one. That's why I never read your message. I stopped reading those notes years ago.

"When I decided to go into real estate, I also decided to keep my two careers separate. That decision was not made to deceive anyone. I wanted to be accepted as a serious person in the real estate community. I wanted clients to see me as a businesswoman, not as a dancer who was selling real estate as a second vocation, or on a whim. It worked, too. No one wrote me silly or disgusting notes. Men treated me with respect. Wives were not threatened by a female agent who seemed more interested in her hairstyle than in the house she was showing."

"Val . . . stop, for just a minute," Rush said hoarsely.

"Let me finish. I know there are many attractive, even glamorous women in real estate. I've met some of them myself." Val tapped her chest with her forefinger. "But I'm talking about me, about what motivated me into dressing plainly, and going without makeup. It was something I felt inside, what I had to do, and until you came along, there was no deceit involved."

Rush moved to the sofa, where he sat with his head down. Val continued standing. "The night we met, the night you came to the company office for the first time, I thought, Rush Saxon is handsome, his clothes are expensive and he's a man to stay away from. Would you like to know why? It's because you weren't the first handsome, expensively dressed man I'd known. I sensed a recklessness about you, and an I'm-just-a-little-bit-better-than-you-are attitude that put me on the defensive."

Rush raised his eyes. "That's not fair, Val."

"Isn't it? Didn't you judge and find me lacking? Didn't you let me know by innuendo if not outright reference that you disapproved of my appearance?"

"I couldn't figure out why you . . ."

"And you let me know it. Rush, I tried to elude anything personal between us. At times I debated telling you about the Casbah, but I kept putting it off because I didn't see any future for us. When things started happening in spite of my reservations, I began worrying about how you might take hearing about my being an entertainer. It would soon be over, I told myself. It would be easier to tell you about it when it was behind me.

"Then Palm Springs happened. We talked about love, and I couldn't ignore my feelings for you any longer. An explanation couldn't be further delayed, although I had already given the Casbah's production manager my notice. I tried to tell you. You have to admit I tried, but by then you had decided I was perfect just as I was, and you didn't want to hear anything that might damage that opinion.

"Oh, I understood what was going on with you, Rush, don't think I didn't. You had decided my preference for unpretentious clothing and an understated appearance had tremendous value. I loved you for it, but can you imagine how I felt trying to come up with a tactful way to tell you that I wasn't the mousy woman you believed I was?"

Val was winding down. A trifle less steady than she'd been, she perched on the edge of a chair. "The day we drove back to Vegas, I realized you had to know. At whatever cost, you *had* to be told. Instead of coming in when we got here, you left with Tom. That was fine. I planned the evening together. I bathed and got ready, and was suddenly exhausted. I lay down for a short nap and woke up hours later. You had called and I slept through the phone ringing. Your message was that you were flying to L.A. with Tom.

"I panicked. You said you'd be back the next day, which was a Tuesday, and I had to go to the Casbah that night. When you called, I tried to impress upon you how important it was that you call me before you came home. I was terrified you'd get here after I left for work and wonder where I was. I hated the idea of telling you something so crucial on the phone, but it would have been better than . . . what happened." She finished in an emotion-filled whisper.

Her speech was apparently over, and its content was careening through Rush's system, touching nerves and his own memory. Needing a minute to digest what he'd heard, to grasp its ramifications, he got up and walked to a window. Outside the sunlight was waning. The eucalyptus and ficus trees cast long shadows on the velvety lawn. A man was walking his dog. The peaceful scene didn't penetrate Rush's concentration.

He turned. "You were very beautiful onstage."

Val took a breath. "Thank you."

"You're very beautiful offstage."

A faint stain of color appeared in her cheeks. "Thank you."

"Do you really think I'm reckless?"

"No, not anymore. That was a first impression and inaccurate."

"And that I think I'm better than other people?"

Val hesitated. "You have a certain... superiority about you."

"Is that bad?" When she didn't immediately answer, he added, "I don't feel superior inside, Val. I especially didn't feel superior when I came to Vegas. I was sick to my stomach scared. I knew nothing about business and had to try."

"I wasn't thinking of business when I said that," Val said quietly. "It's more of a... personal attitude."

"So, on a personal level you see me as what? A snob?"

Val maintained a steady gaze. "I guess that word will do."

"But you're still in love with me, superior, snobbish attitude and all."

She lifted her chin a fraction. "It doesn't seem to be a matter of choice. I didn't want to love you... but I do."

"And I hurt you."

"I hurt you, too," she whispered. "But I never meant to. God, I never meant to," she repeated brokenly. "I was only living out my long-range plan. I had to keep on performing until my real estate career got a decent start. I didn't want the two jobs to overlap, but there just wasn't any other way."

She steadied her voice. "Were you ashamed because I was on the stage that night?"

Rush frowned. "Ashamed?"

"Yes. Were you embarrassed because I was performing publicly?"

Rush's frown deepened as he looked into himself. He remembered the lewd remarks made by the two men at his table, and then the nearly fatal shock of realizing the woman they were lusting after was Val.

"I guess there was some embarrassment involved," he admitted in a low, strained voice. "I'm trying to be honest about it, with you, with myself. What I really felt was betrayed. Stabbed. Lied to."

Val swallowed the lump of tears in her throat. "If I had read your note and met you in the lounge, what would you have said to me?"

Rush raked his hair. "I don't know."

"You were angry."

"Painfully so."

"And outraged."

"Wounded, Val. Ill."

She sat back and sighed, a sorrowful sound. "Fate played a cruel trick on both of us that night. Whatever prompted you to go to the Casbah? I've wondered if Tom said something, even though you insisted he didn't."

"He didn't. I went there by pure accident. When you weren't home, I was too upset to go to bed. I drove around and stopped at the Casbah on impulse." Rush returned to the sofa. Again he sat with his forearms on his knees, leaning forward, his eyes emitting an intense light. "It was all so unnecessary, wasn't it?"

"Yes," she said unsteadily. "A terrible mistake."

They looked at each other across the room. For the first time Rush saw the real Val LeClair. Her luxuriant hair was held back from her beautiful face by two pale pink combs. Her sundress was neither glamorous nor dowdy, a very nice dress that neither emphasized nor disguised her curves. This woman was a mixture of the Val he'd been working with and fallen in love with, and the stunning, flamboyant creature onstage that seemed now, in retrospect, like a dream. Val was the loveliest of chameleons, and she created feelings within himself that no other woman ever had.

He stood up. "I love you. I always will. I'm sorry for hurting you."

She stood up. The tears she'd been battling began spilling down her cheeks. "I'll always love you, all of my life, no matter what else happens. I'm sorry for...everything."

They moved toward each other, spellbound.

Epilogue

The hour was late, the night quiet. Rush was sleeping. Val lay within the circle of his arms, her back to his front, and basked in the glow of undiluted happiness. A miracle had occurred that afternoon. If she had let Rush walk out without conversation, they would not be together now. They would not be planning a wedding, nor would he have said, "You have to meet my brothers. They have to meet you."

She had risked everything: her pride, her dignity, her very soul. Thank God.

There'd been precious little talking once they touched. It was like a dam had burst, with more emotion than Val thought existed in the entire universe. She loved this imperfect man with his air of superiority and unpredictable nature. And, hallelujah, he loved her! She believed it now, truly believed.

Smiling softly, she stretched out a leg that was feeling cramped. Sleeping in a man's arms was not common practice, and maybe that was why she wasn't sleeping at all. But the closeness was wonderful. Soothing, comforting, reassuring.

Rush stirred and mumbled, "Are you awake?"

"Sorry if I woke you."

He made a gratified sound and slid his hand up to her breast. "No problem."

She smiled. But in the next instant she realized that he was becoming very awake. He teased her nipple with his fingertips, and pleasure rippled through her. His head rose from the pillow to press a kiss to the side of her throat. "Want to play?" he whispered.

"Yes," she breathed, closing her eyes.

Playing in the dark was exciting. Rush's hand moved unhurriedly, caressing her breasts until each nipple was upright and achingly sensitized to his touch. He skimmed his fingers down her belly, and her breath caught when he lifted her thigh and draped it over his legs to give him room to explore. Pressed into her behind was the proof of his desire, hard and satiny and moving against her in the most seductive way possible.

"Will you dance for me sometimes?" he whispered huskily as he tormented her most vital spot.

"I'll do anything you want, anytime you say," she gasped.

He chuckled deep in his throat, and warned, "I have a broad imagination, sweetheart."

"So do I, sweetheart," she retorted in a threatening drawl that quickly changed to a moan of sweet pleasure. "Don't stop. Please don't stop."

She was sprawled in a most unladylike manner, spread all over Rush, her legs open, his hand doing magical things to her body. It was fantastic, phenomenal.

His movements were slow and easy, but Val's response was anything but. Tended in such an erotic fashion, she began spinning out of control very quickly. He brought her to the heights, and minutes later, it happened again.

He changed their positions, placing Val on her back. She had become a completely sexual being, and welcomed his penetration with low moans and clutching hands. Her final release, in tune with Rush's, made her weep.

He moved to the bed and held her while she calmed. She finally managed a shaky laugh. "If that was playing, what will happen when you're serious?"

He laughed softly. "You bring out the wild man in me, Valentine."

Ah, so that was it. Smiling knowingly, she teased, "Seeing me onstage did some funny things to you, Mr. Saxon."

He kissed her, passionately. "I'm glad I saw you. What if I never had?"

That idea gave Val pause. "I honestly never thought of that."

He loved her so much, more than he'd ever thought it possible to love anyone. It had happened almost at once for him, he knew now, maybe even that first night in the company office when he'd been surprised to find her there working. What foolish games people play with each other, he thought. He and Val had danced around the obvious, nearly losing each other in the process, merely because their emotions had been unfamiliar and a little frightening.

But it was all behind them now, and thank goodness for that.

Snuggling closer, he brought her hand down to his lap so she would know what was happening to him, because of her. "This is incredible. *You're* incredible," he whispered.

"I think *you* should be written up in the Guinness Book of World Records," Val drawled. They had made love twice before Rush fell asleep, and now this.

"Only if you're in it, too, baby," he whispered, suddenly so hot he had to have her again at once.

It was getting light outside when they stopped "playing." Even their voices were weak as they drifted toward sleep.

Val spoke drowsily. "What about your gold-and-diamond watch, Rush? I know you pawned it."

"I'll get it back, honey. Very soon now."

Contentedly she smiled and turned to another topic that warranted some discussion. "Tom said the Palm Springs project is a go."

"It's coming along great. But I've also got my eye on ten acres right here in Vegas, out on Applegate Road. Know where that is?"

"Approximately. Sounds like you're going to be a big-time developer."

Rush squeezed her closer. "How would you like to be in charge of sales?"

"On your projects?"

"On mine, and on any I might get into with Tom. You and I are a terrific team, sweetheart."

Val's responsive smile faded a little. "Rush, did you ever talk to Tom about your background? I mean, he's a stand-up guy, and..."

"I told him the truth, Val. Just today."

Val sighed. "I'm glad. No one knows better than I just how destructive an omission of information can be." Rush was silent for a long time. "Rush?"

"I did the same thing with Tom that I accused you of doing with me," he said quietly. "Deliberately withheld information. It will never happen again, not with anyone. Val, will you ever be able to forget that it was my mistrust that nearly destroyed what we have?"

She turned over in bed to kiss him. "We love each other. It's over. We'll both forget." She glanced to the window. "The sun's coming up. It's a new day."

"It's a new life," Rush murmured. He nestled her into his arms. "Let's get some sleep."

Val sighed contentedly and snuggled deeper into the bed and Rush's arms. Everything looked rosy now, especially the future.

* * * * *

The Saxon Brothers series continues with Cash's story, PERSISTENT LADY. Look for it in May, from Silhouette Desire.

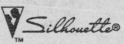

IT'S OUR 1000TH SILHOUETTE ROMANCE, AND WE'RE CELEBRATING!

JOIN US FOR A SPECIAL COLLECTION OF LOVE STORIES
BY AUTHORS YOU'VE LOVED FOR YEARS, AND
NEW FAVORITES YOU'VE JUST DISCOVERED.
JOIN THE CELEBRATION...

April
REGAN'S PRIDE by **Diana Palmer**
MARRY ME AGAIN by **Suzanne Carey**

May
THE BEST IS YET TO BE by **Tracy Sinclair**
CAUTION: BABY AHEAD by **Marie Ferrarella**

June
THE BACHELOR PRINCE by **Debbie Macomber**
A ROGUE'S HEART by **Laurie Paige**

July
IMPROMPTU BRIDE by **Annette Broadrick**
THE FORGOTTEN HUSBAND by **Elizabeth August**

SILHOUETTE ROMANCE...VIBRANT, FUN AND EMOTIONALLY
RICH! TAKE ANOTHER LOOK AT US! AND AS PART OF THE
CELEBRATION, READERS CAN RECEIVE A FREE GIFT!

YOU'LL FALL IN LOVE ALL OVER
AGAIN WITH
SILHOUETTE ROMANCE!

CEL1000

MYSTERY WIFE
Annette Broadrick

She awoke in a French hospital—and found handsome Raoul DuBois, claiming she was his wife, Sherye, mother of their two children. But she didn't recognize him or remember her identity. Whoever she was, Sherye grew more attached to the children every day—and the growing passion between her and Raoul was like nothing they'd ever known before....

She's friend, wife, mother—she's you! And beside each Special Woman stands a wonderfully *special* man. It's a celebration of our heroines—and the men who become part of their lives.

Don't miss THAT SPECIAL WOMAN! each month— from some of your special authors! Only from Silhouette Special Edition!

TSW494